DINKWEED

Copyright © 2021 by A.G. Reidy. All rights reserved.

You are welcome to print a copy of this document for your personal use. Other than that, no part of this publication may be reproduced, stored, or transmitted in any form or by any means, electronic, mechanical, photocopying, recording, scanning, or otherwise, except as permitted under Section 107 or 108 of the 1976 United States Copyright Act, without the prior written permission of the author.

For Ma and Dad:

Thank you for this life, love and for teaching us

the importance of family!

CONTENTS

PREFACE

So…here we are again!

I'll start this off with a warning! If you didn't like the first *dinkweed* book, save your money, because you won't like this one either!

This book is more of the same – silly, nostalgic stories and shenanigans that follow "Gary" and his brothers through the streets of Lowell, MA during the 1970's.

Like book one, it is not politically correct and reads like the times in which it is set. If you are offended by adolescent shenanigans or words, again, you might want to buy a different book. No hard feelings, but don't blame me if you proceed.

Now, if you are still here: Thank you!

A few things happened on my way to this second book. As most of my fans, or "dinkweeds" as you are now affectionately referred to on my Facebook page know, I had never even planned on writing a first book, let alone a second one. I still don't consider myself a great writer, but I have conceded I can tell a pretty good story that might keep you a little bit interested. I base this on the fact that I sold more than the twenty books I had hoped to sell and picked up some awesome fans. I never expected the support I've received or that so many people would connect with it like they have. I've been asked by a number of dinkweeds when would I write book two. It became something in the back of my mind as a "maybe."

That changed though, and I'd like to tell you what gave me the final push.

Call it divine intervention.

A very sweet childhood friend and fan reached out to me privately. She was very ill —more ill than I had realized at the time. She asked me to please write a second book. She said that her and her husband, the love of her life, were going through a lot of stress and trying to stay positive through her illness. She told me that one of the bright spots in the midst of this was my first book. She said that it made her so happy to see him laugh so hard when he was reading it. He is from the same area and could personally identify and recognize a few of the characters. It gave him a happy nostalgic feeling. She said she would really appreciate it if I wrote a second book.

I told her I would and started to focus on it more.

A few months later I received the sad news that she had passed away. I reached out to her husband to offer my condolences and he said maybe if I ever wrote a second book, I could name a character after her. It could be in any of the stories, and it would be great if she was mentioned in the book.

What I found ironic and sweet about this, was that they had both asked me separately and unknowingly to do something for the other. What a testament of the love they had for each other. She wanted him laughing, and he wanted her remembered.

When I relayed this story to my husband, he smiled and said, "now you have no excuse not to write another book."

I hope I've done right by their requests.

So, here I am. And here we are.

Just like the first book, every story has a bone of truth running right down the center—wrapped in a muscle of bullshit. I'll never tell what the bone is or which character it really belongs to. I've changed names and places for privacy. If you recognize a person, place, or event, it may be merely coincidental. I'll leave that up to you to decide and will neither confirm nor deny.

This second *dinkweed* novel picks up two months after the drive-in. Gary and Mary are now freshmen in high school.

Like the first book, other than the first and last chapter, there is no chronological order. You can pick it up, skip around, and just read. I've heard it's a good beach read and a great bathroom book (I think that's a compliment!).

Unlike the first book, this time I give a few of the characters a chance to have their own chapter narrated by them. Gary will still be the main story teller, but a few of the other characters have their moments. I'd also like to point out, as I've mentioned before: this book is based on my brothers. My sister and myself play a side role—the characters though, are a combination of us and other people depending on the subject.

If you were entertained by the first book, I hope this book leaves you feeling the same way.

This will, however, be the last *dinkweed* book. I don't want the characters to get older than this. Once they start having sex, it's just not as funny anymore!

You may see a *dinkweed Halloween Stories* or a *dinkweed cookbook* or something similar down the line, but after this book, I'll sadly let the boys grow up (although they never really have!). Of course, this could all change if *dinkweed* is ever picked up for a T.V. Series! (A girl can dream, can't she?)

Once again, I'd like to thank my siblings, friends, and cousins for these stories. Without their humor and shenanigans, we would have lived a boring life. I'm beyond blessed to have them all in my life. They are exceptional people, and I thank God for them every day.

I want to thank all of you for your support, encouragement, and for spreading the word about the book. The photos you sent of the many places around the world you read *dinkweed* meant a lot, too. I'd also like to give a big thank you to those of you who donated to the causes that *dinkweed* supports: Suicide prevention, our veterans, End 68 Hours of Hunger, and to local food banks—no one should ever be alone or hungry.

Through *dinkweed*, I've made new connections and have re-connected with old friends. This has meant more to me than you will ever know. I now consider you my friends, and I love and thank you all.

So, grab a chair, a bowl of radish, and a Schlitz! Thanks, again, for the support. And remember, it's not Shakespeare folks, it's just *dinkweed*!

Amy

"THEY CAN TAKE MY HOUSE, BUT NEVER MY
HOME OR MY MEMORIES. THOSE BELONG TO ME."

C. GOAD

BROTHERS

"Gary, are you listening to anything I just said?" Mary was getting aggravated now.

"Yes, of course I am!"

I wasn't though—we were at Pizza Town, the after-school joint we all hung out at. It was either there or Rick's for a burger, and today we wanted pizza. We were each having a slice, a salad, and a Coke. "Band on the Run" was playing on the jukebox and she had that green sweater on that I loved. I couldn't focus on anything else.

Mary and I were freshman in high school now, and we've been going together since August when we went to the drive-in to see *Grease*. After two months, I've still seen no boob. I tried once a few weeks ago. We were making out in my back yard; my brothers were playing catch and I told them to beat it. (It was me who ended up beating it though, if you get the picture!).

I tried to go for it, and Mary told me, "Gary, I'm not Shelly! Knock it off. I'm not ready for that stuff yet."

I guess I like her enough to wait, maybe I even love her, but man, if she's gonna keep wearing that green sweater…

10

"GARY!!!" she raised her voice and jolted me out of my thoughts. "What are you gonna do about it?"

"Do about what, Mar?" I sighed.

"See, I knew you weren't listening. I'll say it one more time. Michael, Angie, and the gang were playing Relievio the other night. Your dad was in your bathroom, and Michael asked if he could use ours to pee. Since that night, I can't find my back-scratcher-washer-stick-thing! I know he took it, and I want you to ask him about it. It's creepy!"

"What would he want with that?" I asked.

"That's what I need you to find out," she stressed.

I told her I'd find out if the little freak took it.

She softened a bit now, "okay, thanks. Hey, I have to babysit for the Coopers on Saturday. Wanna come over for a while with me?"

I hated the Coopers. The guy was a creep who grabbed Aunt Marie's ass once at a house party, and Dad bent his finger so hard he almost broke it.

I sat wondering how he'd feel about me coming over. I liked that it might make him feel weird.

"Only if you make it worth my while." She shot me a look. I said, "yeah, I'll come. What time?" I was holding out hope for the ever-elusive boob grab.

We finished eating and walked over the bridge holding hands. When we got to the other side, I saw Aaron surrounded by a group of kids from a few streets over.

I've seen this before, and I knew what this was.

Once again, Aaron, the little shit, shot his mouth off and was gonna get an ass kicking.

Mary looked at me and whispered, "do something."

I stopped and put my finger up to my mouth looking at Mary. We stood there for a minute, unnoticed.

"YOU LITTLE FUCKER! I'M GONNA BEAT YOUR ASS, YOU LITTLE DICK!" the biggest one in the group yelled at Aaron.

"LITTLE DICK, YEAH THAT SOUNDS LIKE SOMETHING THAT WOULD COME RIGHT OUTTA YOUR MOUTH," Aaron yelled back.

This kid had some balls. Four guys to his one, and he was still mouthing off. I had a good mind to let it happen, but knew I just couldn't do that. As usual, I could kick Aaron's ass—and have on many occasions—but no one else had that right.

As the bigger kid advanced towards Aaron, one of the other guys noticed me. I had let go of Mary's hand and had my arms at my sides. My fists were all balled up ready to punch, and I had a look to kill on my face.

He elbowed the guy next to him. The elbows made their way around the circle without Aaron even noticing until the biggest kid suddenly changed his tune.

"I'm only shitting with you, Aaron. And good one about the dick thing! We're cool. See ya later," he said. And with that, they scattered.

Aaron stood there a minute, puffed up his chest, and yelled, "YEAH, YOU BET YOUR ASS WE'RE COOL, YOU ASSWIPES."

He started walking towards home all proud of himself. I stood my ground, and grabbed Mary's hand to let him get a good distance ahead.

No one in the neighborhood would really mess with him right now. I had a reputation of being a tough guy, so most of the kids didn't want trouble with me. Me and Mary had that in common.

Mary wasn't really tough, and I don't think I've ever seen her get in a fight, but she was forever having to come to Angie's defense. As a result, the younger girls were intimated by her. Angie had a big mouth sometimes, like Aaron, with nothing to back it up, except for Mary.

Mary leaned in as Aaron walked away and asked, "aren't you gonna say something to him?"

"Nah, let the little dinkweed enjoy it while he can. One day I won't be here, and he'll probably get that ass kicking he deserves. Let him enjoy it now," I said as I started walking.

Mary tugged on my hand, pulled me back, and faced me. "And that is why you are my boyfriend, Gary," she said as she planted a kiss on me. We walked the rest of the way home not talking. I was fine with that.

When I got home, Ma was folding laundry.

"Where's Michael?" I asked.

"He's upstairs in his room reading his comic book. He just got back from Vinnie's," she answered without looking up.

Vinnie's Comic Store was a few blocks over from our house. They sold all the latest and greatest comics: Monsters, Fangoria, Marvel, and DC comics. Anything you wanted. It was one of our favorite places.

Vinnie would let you hang out there for hours looking through the inventory of comic books, but you had to let him frisk you before you left. If you didn't, you'd be barred for life. He never did anything pervy or I'da busted him one. He would make you turn your front pockets out, hit your ass with the back of his hand, and make you lift up your pant legs and shirt. As long as you agreed to the frisk at the end, you could hang out there for a while.

Vinnie's was usually the only place where Michael would spend any money. He would read his comics with carefully washed hands, and then wrap them in plastic. He said they were an "investment." Then he'd hide them. I didn't care enough to go looking for them, and Aaron was too busy learning new tricks on his bike. So, his books were safe…for now.

I ran up the stairs taking two at a time. When I walked in the room, Mike was on his bottom bunk bed reading *Dr. Strange*.

"Hey, dinkweed, stand up. I gotta talk to you."

"What do I have to stand up for? I'm reading right now," he said.

I leaned in and told him, "stand up, or I touch the book with my greasy paws—that's why!"

He put the book to his side and stood up.

"Okay, listen, I'm gonna only ask you this once, and if you lie, you're gonna get it 'cause I already know the truth." (I didn't). "Did you or did you not take Mary's back-scratcher-brush-thing from her bathroom?"

Mike opened his mouth to say something as I held him against the door. I held up a finger and said, "WAIT. Think about your answer before you say it 'cause if it's a lie, you're getting a punch."

We both stood there for a minute quietly staring each other down until he cracked. "Okay, okay. Yeah, I took it," he admitted.

"Now, why the fuck did you do something like that for? You little freak. Where is it?"

That question was an important one because if it was anywhere within whacking off distance, like under his mattress or the side of the bed, he was getting a punch anyway.

"I don't have it anymore," he offered.

"What do you mean? When did you last have it?"

He lowered his eyes and said, "I sold it to my buddy, Tim, for $5.00."

"WHY?" I asked as my grip tightened.

"He has always had a crush on Mary. He knows she's older and that she loves you. So, he'd never get her. He asked me to take it because he heard Angie and his sister, Donna, talking about it and how they wanted one. He said he wouldn't do anything weird with it—"

"Yeah, right!" I thought.

"He said he'd just shower with it," Michael continued. "So, he asked me to get it for him for $5.00. I needed the money for comics, and so I did it," he confessed.

"Needed the money! Mike, you have more money around here than anyone."

"I know, but that's my point of no return money that I don't touch. So, it's kinda like I have no money," he reasoned.

I thought about this for a minute. "I gotta tell ya, kid, I don't know whether your nuts or if I'm impressed. Anyway, you gotta make this right."

"Want me to get it back?" he offered.

"HELL, NO! God knows what Tim's done with it already." I'd deal with him later. "But you are gonna give me half of that money plus another buck for my silence. As far as Mary knows, you never took it! Got it?" I threatened.

Truth be told, it was me who needed to worry. If Mary found out I knew and took money related to the thievery, she'd be bullshit.

"But I told you: I have no money! I spent it on the comic books," Mike said dejected.

"Well, guess what, dinkweed? $3.50 just came back from the point of no return money! Give it to me by tomorrow."

I left the room thinking that between him and Aaron, I've had enough of those two for the day.

I showed up on Tim's porch ten minutes later. He was sitting out drinking a root beer when I turned up. He made a move to run in the house, and I grabbed him by the back of the shirt. "Where do you think you're going?!"

Visibly shaken, he said, "you look mad, so I wanna go in."

"Mad isn't the half of it, Tim. You're lucky I don't wipe the floor with you right now. Go, get me the brush, NOW!"

I barely got the words out of my mouth when Tim ran into the house. He was out in less than thirty seconds.

He handed me the brush, "I won't do something like this again, Gary. Come on, don't beat the crap out of me. I'm good friends with your brother."

I eyeballed him for a minute while he stood there shaking, and I thought he might shit his pants.

"I'll tell ya what I'm gonna do. You caught me in a good mood. I won't tell Mary you took it. I'll cut you a break because Michael likes you. Know this though," I said while squeezing his cheeks, "you mention this to anyone or ever do anything like this again, and I'll give you a beating worse than you would have got today. AND you can give me $5.00 like you gave Mike. I want it by next week."

"I promise, Gar, I promise and thanks. Boy Scouts honor," he said as he held up three fingers. I almost busted out laughing.

"Don't thank me, because in addition to all this, you will owe me one. I'll let you know when you have to repay me." It was always good to have something to hold over someone's head. You never knew when you'd need it.

I left the porch and heard his door slam behind me.

19

I pitched the back-scratcher-brush-thing in the first garbage barrel I saw on my way home where it would never be found.

"$8.50!" I thought, "not a bad haul for a Monday."

MICHAEL

Not gonna lie, I was glad that Gary went to the high school now. I hated him being in the same school with me for two reasons. First, I'd catch so much shit from teachers expecting me to be just like him. The other, more important reason, was now he couldn't go to the junior high dances anymore. No more toe nail humiliation. Bastard.

Being in the eighth grade now, I was in a position to rag on the lower grades. That wasn't my style though. I wasn't the "loves a good fight" guy, like Gary, or the "big mouth," like Aaron, but what I didn't do in those areas, I made up for in smarts.

I could definitely hold my own in a fight—and have—if I had to. Don't get me wrong, Gary was wicked smart, so was Aaron for that matter, but neither of them figured out yet how to take another route.

Between Gary's fist and Aaron's mouth they didn't have to. I found out a long time ago how to use my brains to my own advantage though. No one ever messed with me. Part of that I know had to do with Gary, but the other was because I learned one common sense thing the other two hadn't quite mastered yet.

21

Keep your fucking mouth shut—you don't always have to open it.

You can stand back instead and hardly anyone notices you at all. This was fine with me. I didn't have time for the same shit that everyone else did.

I had a plan.

I rarely got yelled at by Dad because every night after dinner, I put my plate in the sink without being told. Every Sunday night, I brought the one barrel I was responsible for to the curb. It was so simple, yet so difficult for the other two.

Many a Monday morning, I'd hear the old man flipping out: "HEY, PECKERHEADS! GET OUT HERE AND BRING YOUR BARRELLS OUT. MICHEAL IS THE ONLY ONE WHO DID!"

I'd see the other two stumble out of bed in their underwear, go outside like that, and drag their barrels to the street.

They'd be all pissed off when they'd come back inside, and Gary would say, "stop being such a kiss ass. You are making us look bad."

I'd tell him, "Gar, I'm not a kiss ass—I just know the old man is gonna flip the fuck out, and I don't feel like hearing it so I

22

beat him to the punch. If you'd use your head, you'd figure that out."

Gary would usually lean over and give me a charley horse at this point, and the conversation was over until next Sunday or after dinner when Dad would yell for the plates to be brought out to the sink.

"Your mother is not a maid. TAKE OUT YOUR PLATE!" he'd holler. Followed two seconds later with, "hey, Carole, get me a beer would ya?"

Don't get me wrong, just because I used my head a little more doesn't mean I still didn't have my brothers blood running through me. I could still be talked into a few things, especially where Gary was concerned.

He always made everything ridiculous sound entirely logical. Anything I knew about girls, for instance, I learned from him, who in turn learned from Frank next door.

Frank was a wealth of knowledge. Maybe not the knowledge Ma would be happy with us learning but knowledge none the less.

This brings me to last Friday night.

I was sitting in the back yard with my buddy, John, having a coke and thinking of what to do when Gary and my cousin, Billy, walked in. We were having an important conversation about the new movie, *Halloween*, that was coming out, and how would we get tickets to see it. It was rated-R, and none of us were old enough to get in without an adult. Plus, we needed the ride to the Rte. 3 Cinema. We both knew Ma and Dad wouldn't be interested in seeing it, so we couldn't talk them into taking us.

Then, just like fucked up magic, Frank appeared at the fence a few houses over. Surprisingly, he had on pants this time. Franks usual attire was a butt hanging out of his mouth, a beer belly, and boxers. We weren't used to seeing him in pants. He had been listening to our conversation.

"Hey, dinkweed. If you wanna go see that shit, all you have to do is ask me to take you."

"Really?" I asked "Okay, will you take us?"

"Fuck, no," he said followed by a loud burp. "But thanks for asking, shithead."

"Muthafucka," I thought, but of course didn't say out loud.

"Hey, come on over here the four of you," he said.

"Why?" I asked still annoyed.

"Calm down, calm down. I'll take you idiots to see the stupid movie, but I need you guys to come here. You guys know how to play cards?"

"A little poker," Gary answered.

Uncle Sammy and Dad played poker sometimes on Saturday fish fry nights, and they had taught us how to play to make it a bigger game for them. Which by the way, they had no guilt about winning our allowance money.

"Perfect," Frank said. "Meet me at the back door."

We all walked over. Gary said, "last time Frank told us to come to the back door, it was to see a naked girl." He was hoping for the same.

Frank was standing there, and as he removed his butt from his mouth, he whispered, "I picked up these chicks—they wanna play poker, and I'm the only guy in there. I need more guys."

Gary perked up, "this wouldn't be strip poker would it, Frank?"

"Wait, wait," said John, "I'm not gonna have to take off my clothes, am I?"

25

Frank just smiled and said, "don't worry, they'll never see your hairless sack. I'm gonna get things started. I'll cheat a little at first so my clothes come off—that'll loosen things up. I only need you guys in there so I can get something going with them. It shouldn't take long; they seem pretty free and easy. Then you can leave. None of you are getting naked. Now come on in boys, and try not to act like the morons that ya are. Be cool."

As he put his hand on the door, he turned towards us and said, "don't embarrass me. If you do, you'll get an ass kicking after I'm done with these chicks."

When we went inside there were three girls sitting at the table. They were cute girls: Two blondes and a brunette, they all looked about twenty, had big jugs, and long Farrah Fawcett hair. Frank was twenty-three now, so I'm sure he was in heaven over scoring these younger, hot chicks. How he got them all to come over for strip poker by himself was soon made apparent.

"I thought you said you had a bunch of hot friends to play with us, too," the cute brunette was pissed.

"I do," Frank answered.

"But these are little boys! What the fuck!" one of the blondes piped in.

"Relax, ladies, relax. They may look little, but they know what they are doing," he said.

"We do?" my buddy, John, whispered to me.

"Besides, all my other friends are busy. They'll have to do," Frank continued.

With that, Frank grabbed a six pack out of the fridge, lit a joint, and said, "come, ladies. We are all here for a good time. Drink and smoke up!" He took a beer for himself and gave each of the girls one, which seemed to make them feel better. Then, he passed one to me and one to Gary and whispered, "you two share yours with your two buddies. I don't need you little shits getting drunk over here—your dad will kill me."

"Are you fucking kidding me," Gary whispered as he passed the beer, "no problem showing us a naked girl, but now he's all concerned about giving us all a beer. It's bullshit! He's just being cheap and using us." Which truth be told, Gary was fine with, and for that matter so were the rest of us. We were all hoping to get a peek at these girls.

We all sat around the table. As the joint made its way around, one of the girls said, "don't pass it to the boys. They shouldn't be smoking—they are too little." (Again, too little to smoke, but okay to have a beer and play strip poker). So, the joint went on by us.

Frank picked up the deck and started to deal.

As a show of good faith, before the game got under way, everyone took off one article of clothing and threw it in the pot. Me, the boys, and two of the girls all put in a sock.

John's sock was cruddy and black, and one of the girls said "EWWW!" Gary just looked at him, and shook his head and said, "you couldn't have chosen something else?"

Frank put in his shirt, and then a blonde girl took off her shirt and threw it on the pile. She had on a white bra with her big boobs, and said, "I figured this would help keep it interesting."

We all sat there staring at her when Frank smacked my cousin, Billy, upside the head and said, "pick up your cards, dinkweed."

We started to play.

Every hand for the first three games Frank "lost." As we finished the fourth game, Cindy, the cute brunette, lost her vest. On the fifth game, Frank lost again, and he reached down and threw his boxers into the pile. "Well, ladies, there's nothing to it! Let's continue to play. I'll just be dealer."

As they agreed, we began to get excited because with him as naked dealer, this meant others were going to lose their clothes. We knew that Frank didn't want it to be us.

Just as he finished dealing the cards and put the joint once again to his mouth, we heard the front door slam, and his mother walked into the front room screaming, "MOVE YOUR FRIGGING CAR, FRANCIS!"

When Frank didn't answer, she walked into the kitchen. She took a look around, assessing the situation and yelled, "WHAT IN THE HELL IS GOING ON IN HERE?"

Me and the boys sat there frozen, the girls jumped up saying, "sorry, sorry." While they scrambled to grab their clothes from the pile. As soon as she took in the scene, she flipped out.

"FRANCIS WALTER, WHAT IN THE HELL IS GOING ON?! IT SMELLS LIKE MARIJANA, AND THERE IS ALCOHOL, HALF NAKED WOMEN, AND MINORS IN HERE!"

His mum continued her rant while Frank just sat there quietly. We sat there frozen.

"LEAVE THIS HOUSE!!!" she screamed at all of us. The girls ran out the door quickly. She walked up behind me and

Billy, and smacked us upside the back of the head. "IDIOTS! GET THE HELL OUT!"

We weren't sure what to do because she was still standing there right behind us, and we had nowhere to run.

"FRANCIS WALTER, STAND UP AND PUT THAT MAJURANIA IN THE BARRELL. I DON'T WANT TO LOOK AT IT OR SMELL IT!!!" she yelled with her face turning red.

Again, Frank just sat there quietly.

"DID YOU HEAR ME? STAND UP, NOW, I SAID!"

Frank answered calmly, "I can't, Ma."

"WHY NOT? GET UP. RIGHT NOW!"

Frank looked at her calmly, put the joint down, and slowly stood up, "I'm naked, Ma."

We saw our opportunity as she lunged at him across the table. As we ran out the door, all we could hear was, "YOU ARE OUT, MISTER! THIS TIME I MEAN IT: OUT!"

That wasn't the first time Frank would be thrown out or the last.

Frank never did leave though. He'd always kiss her ass for a while and wait it out. She'd always forgive him and tell my mum sometimes when they'd be talking across the fence, "Oh, my Frankie is a bugga! I'd be lost without him though."

I guess Frank had that effect on some people!

We all had a good laugh about it the following Saturday when he took us all to see *Halloween* at the cinema. Of course, not before we paid him with gas and beer money.

Some things never change.

HUFFY

One night, I walked in the front door after spending twenty minutes saying good night to Mary. Ma was frantic, it was 9 o'clock—two hours after the street lights went on and Aaron wasn't home yet.

"Gary, I need you to go look for Aaron. No one knows where he is. I just called Aunt Marie, and she is having Billy look around their neighborhood for him. Please go take a look around for him. He's never home this late, and he never even came home for dinner."

I told her I'd go and I grabbed the flashlight on my way out. For the next hour I walked up and down the streets, calling out his name. This kid was gonna get it when I got my hands on him.

I ended up at the end of Main Street near the bridge.

As I was approaching the bridge, I saw Aaron at the other end. He was pushing his bike and heading towards me from the other side of town. The part my folks had told him he wasn't allowed to go to alone—especially after dark.

"You are FUCKING DEAD!" I was pissed. "Where the hell have you been, and what were you doing over there?"

He stopped pushing his bike and stood there just looking at me.

"Move!" I said while grabbing him by the shirt. Truth be told, I was relieved to see him. After looking around for the last hour, I was starting to get nervous thinking something could have really happened to the little shit this time. Aaron was mouthy and although he had proved he was pretty good at taking care of himself, he wasn't even eleven yet.

He pushed his bike, and we walked in silence. We cut through the back street towards the park at the end of our street.

"Stop. Sit down here for a minute. I want to hear where you were before we get home," I said motioning towards the bench.

"I don't wanna tell ya 'cause you're gonna punch me," he said.

"Dinkweed, it might be to your advantage 'cause if it's a good reason, I'll back you up," I countered.

"It is a good reason. Promise you won't punch me first? Give me your word," he said still standing.

I thought about this a minute. I knew as soon as I said I give my word, I had to. If Dad got involved, he'd make sure I did. "You make a promise you keep a promise, PERIOD" was Dad's motto.

"Okay, I promise," I answered.

He sat down.

This was the story.

I knew that Aaron had made a deal with my folks. He really wanted a Huffy Thunder Road Bike, but at $100.00 a pop there was no way he could afford it. He was too young to work and didn't have his own paper route. He could get me and Mike to sometimes let him take a day or two on ours but that wasn't enough. He talked my parents into going in half with him for his birthday if he could come up with his half. They agreed.

It took Aaron six months of no allowance, extra chores, helping out old lady Moran at the top of the street with yard work, and a few days of the paper route to save up his $50. But he did it.

From the moment he got that bike, it was love at first sight. He told me he'd spend all day practicing moves and jumps.

He only had it a month, when today, he turned the corner from his walk home from school and saw his buddy, John, running up the street.

"Aaron, where's your bike?" he yelled.

"It's chained up in the back yard. What's going on?" he asked while running towards our yard.

John told him he had just seen Hector Mino (an older kid who lived in the projects on the other side of the bridge) ride by the 24-hour store on a bike that looked just like his.

Aaron panicked as he ran in the yard to discover the chain was cut, and the bike was gone.

He was so pissed that without saying a word to anyone, he took off towards the bridge.

When he got to the tenements on the other side, he said there were a group of guys standing in a circle. He asked them which apartment was Hector's.

"Who wants to know?" the biggest one answered.

Aaron told him, "I want to know; he stole my bike and I want it back."

They all started to laugh, and the big one answered, "oh, and you are just gonna go knock on his door and tell him that? This I gotta see! He lives at number three."

When Aaron knocked on the door, the group stood behind him.

A big man with muscles and a white t-shirt and jeans answered the door. When he told Aaron Hector wasn't home, Aaron said, "sir, can I talk to you a minute?"

The man studied him and looked at the group of boys behind him and told them, "get the hell out of here. Take off." They scattered.

"Come inside, little man, and tell me what this is all about."

Aaron followed him in.

"HE WENT INSIDE!" I thought with my head exploding, but I just sat there and let him finish his story.

Aaron told me that he told the man, Mr. Mino, about how hard he worked to save that money for his half of the bike and how Ma and Dad don't have much either, and it was hard for them to save their half. He told him how he liked to do tricks on the bike and how stealing is wrong, and Hector had no right. He said he was spitting mad at the last part and had his fists balled up when he said it.

Mr. Mino looked at him for a few minutes. Then, he said over his shoulder, "Maria, I'll be back in a while." Then he said to Aaron, "follow me, little man."

For the next four hours, Mr. Mino took Aaron all over town. They walked from one block to another knocking on different doors and going into different back yards. The first place they went, they collected the handlebars of his bike. At the second place, they found the body of the bike. The tires where at another place. Until, finally, they found the chain and the seat in different place.

Everywhere they went they were told, "you just missed Hector." But everyone passed the goods over to Mr. Mino with no questions asked and no argument.

When they walked back to Mr. Mino's house with all the parts, he opened the front door and yelled for Hector.

Hector was home, came to the door, and looked at Aaron and his father standing there with all the parts he had just sold. He looked scared.

"Get out here!" Mr. Mino said as he walked over to him. He grabbed Hector by the shirt. "You stole this kid's bike," he said through gritted teeth.

Hector looked down and said, "yes, sir."

Mr. Mino stared at him for a few seconds and said, "I'll deal with that later. Right now, go inside get me a beer, my tool box, and get back out here. You are going to put this whole bike back together. And don't tell me you don't know how 'cause you sure as hell knew how to take it all apart! Now move."

Mr. Mino sat on the steps drinking his beer with Aaron next to him while Hector started putting the bike back together. When it came time to put the chain on, Aaron jumped up to help him since it was a hard job for one person.

When the bike was assembled, Hector stood up and Mr. Mino got off the steps and walked over to him. "You got something you want to say to him?"

Hector looked at Aaron and said, "I am sorry I took it. I shouldn't have."

"Yeah, you shouldn't have is right," Mr. Mino interjected. "You could learn a thing or two from this little man," he said while patting Aaron on the back.

"Well, anyway, I mean it," Hector said while putting out his hand for Aaron to shake.

Aaron said he was less pissed and more relieved to have his bike back, so he shook Hector's hand.

Mr. Mino told Aaron not to be a stranger as he got on his bike. Aaron told him thank you and he wouldn't be, but told me he was thinking he'd never be back because he realized he was hours late getting home. The street lights were on and Dad was probably going to kill him anyway.

When Aaron was finished his story, I sat there thinking, "Jesus, this kid is nuts. But he does have a set of balls on him."

"So, that's the truth, Gary. That's where I was," he said.

"Aaron, do you have any idea how incredibly fucking bad this whole thing could have gone?"

"Well, I got my bike back!" Aaron smiled.

I put my hand on his shoulder and said, "let's get going. Ma is probably going crazy."

Just as I expected, as soon as we walked in the door, Ma charged into the front room. "Aaron!! Where have you been we've been worried sick?!"

Dad came barreling in and got right in Aaron's face, "you better have a good excuse. You made your mother a nervous wreck!" he hissed.

Before Aaron could answer, I blurted out, "he's a moron. He was with Mark, his buddy from school. They went to his house and were watching T.V. and playing games and stuff. He said he lost track of time."

"Lost track of time! Listen, dumbass, maybe you won't lose track of time again if you don't have your bike for a week! How about that?" Dad yelled.

"Sorry, Dad. I promise I won't ever let it happen again." Aaron said quietly.

"You're right. You won't. Now get up to bed. I don't care if you are hungry," Dad yelled.

Aaron started up the stairs, and I went up behind him. When we got to our room, Aaron said, "thanks for covering for me, Gary. Dad flipped out thinking I was just at a friend's house. I don't want to know what he would have done if I told him what really happened."

"Don't thank me, Aaron. I only covered for you because you took care of it yourself. Telling them the truth would have given Ma a heart attack. Next time something like that happens and you don't come to me first, I'll kick the living shit out of you. Got it?"

"Got it," he said.

We shook on it.

I passed Ma on my way back downstairs, she had a glass of milk in her hand and a peanut butter and jelly sandwich on a napkin for Aaron. She just couldn't help herself!

POETRY IN MOTION

When I walked in from school on Wednesday afternoon, Ma greeted me from the kitchen.

"What did you do Gary? What trouble have you got yourself into now?" I could tell she was pissed.

"Ma, what are you talking about? I didn't do anything," I said.

"I just got a call from your housemaster, Mr. Sanchez. He wants to have a meeting with me tomorrow morning. What did you do?" She stood there with her hand on her hip waiting for a response.

"Honest to God, Ma, I can't think of anything," I said. "Well, anything recent," I thought.

I know a few months ago I got into trouble because my accounting teacher said I was too argumentative with him. I told him I'd like to debate that if I could. He called me a wise guy, and so I said I wanted to object to that as well. But Ma already knew about that. I served a night of detention for that already. Since then, I'd taken a vow of silence in his class. Now, whenever he asks me a question, I either stand up and act out the answer like a mime or I use made up sign language. When he told me my way of responding was annoying, I wrote "YOU

41

CAN'T HAVE IT BOTH WAYS" on a piece of paper and held it up to him. He didn't even give me detention for that—I think he was grateful for my silence.

Ma snapped me out of my thinking. "Well, if it's something bad, Gary, I'll have to tell your father. You'd be better off telling me now."

"Ma, your guess is as good as mine," I said.

Later on, Mary and I were sitting on the couch discussing it between a few kisses.

"Come on, Gary, you know what you did," she said.

"I don't, Mary—honestly."

"What? Too many things to choose from? You know it's not easy defending some of the crap you and Billy have done," she said.

"We just try to keep things exciting, Mary, that's all," I said defensively.

"Oh, like the time in art class when Mrs. Reed said we all had to do an art presentation and you and Billy teamed up and acted out Norman Rockwell paintings?" she said.

"Oh, come on, Mary, you laughed," I said. Then, I started laughing when I remembered us acting out the "Apple for the

Teacher" painting. I remembered playing the part of the student, bent over with my ass sticking up, offering the overly surprised teacher (Billy) an apple. We did five more interpretations.

"You guys are dopes sometimes," Mary laughed.

"Well, Mrs. Reed gave us a B+. She said she was going to give us an A until we did the "Pin Up Girl" painting and smooshed our chest together to make cleavage. She said it was inappropriate" I rebutted.

"Okay, well, I guess it's a better grade than the one you dinkweeds got in music class. Remember that time when you had to pick out a musician or singer and tell everyone how the music made you feel? You two picked Frank Sinatra and the song "That's Why the Lady Is a Tramp," and then blew bubbles. Mrs. Murphy said the bubbles were a nice touch, but she wanted you to verbalize how the song makes you feel. And so, you both stood up, and at the same time said, "HORNY!" loudly. She was pissed!"

"She had no sense of humor, Mary. And besides, that song kinda does make me horny," I told her.

"You are something else," she said swatting at me. "Anyway, Gary, I don't think you know what Mr. Sanchez wants to talk to your mother about because there are probably too many things to choose from," she said laughing.

I'm sure I'd find out what it was tomorrow.

We went back to kissing.

The next day when I came home from school, I walked into the kitchen and Ma and Aunt Marie were sitting at the kitchen table having coffee.

"Sit down, Gary," Ma said seriously.

I sat. "Okay, Ma, let me have it. What did I do?"

"Okay, Gary, I will tell you this: It's not all bad. Mr. Sanchez and your journalism teacher were both in on the meeting," she started.

"OH, OH!" I thought, a light just went on. I said nothing. Ma told me the meeting went something like this:

Mr. Sanchez introduced the journalism teacher, Mrs. Wood to Ma.

He gave the floor to her.

"Okay, Mrs. Simpson, let me start out by saying I don't know if you are aware of how talented Gary is with his writing and journalism skills. He's got a good grasp of the English language and is very inquisitive which is a great quality to have as a future journalist. I've spoken to his English teacher and we've shared articles and stories he's submitted. Although somewhat disturbing in nature, he wrote a very good story for the Halloween edition of the school paper this past October. I'd like to give you a copy to read at your leisure." She slid the story over to Ma.

It was called "Retribution".

"We'd like to point out to you that he has an A- in both of our classes. It would be an A+ if not for his shenanigans. Gary likes to push the envelope. We've overlooked a number of things; however, this last one was something we couldn't ignore."

She went on to explain.

"Every Monday, my journalism class is assigned to write some articles and stories of interest to be passed in on Fridays. I then sign off on them and submit them to the school newspaper for publication and distribution the following Tuesday. In light of Robert Frost's recent birthday, we decided to have a poetry section in the centerfold of the newspaper. Well, to cut to the chase, Mrs. Simpson, Gary wrote two poems, forged my signature, and submitted them without my knowledge."

She continued, "here is a copy of Tuesdays paper that was distributed to every single student and faculty member at the school. Please turn to the centerfold for the special section on poems."

Ma said she opened it, and among other poems about life and birds and trees, she found the following two poems by me.

"S.O.B"
By Gary Simpson
Fire, fire, false alarm.
Baby shit in sisters' arm,
Brother went to pull the switch,
And baby said, "you son of a bitch!"

"Poems on a Wall"
By Gary Simpson
He who writes on shit house walls,
Rolls his shit in little balls.
He who reads these words of wit,
Will eat the little balls of shit.

Ma said she sat there with her mouth hanging open.

"So, you see, Mrs. Simpson, our predicament. We don't want to discourage Gary's talents; however, we cannot abide by this inappropriate behavior. We are going to give him three days of in-house suspension, and make him write an apology in next week's paper. We also ask that you please speak with him at home about his behavior."

"That is more than fair, Mr. Sanchez and Mrs. Wood. I greatly apologize on Gary's behalf, and I can assure you he will get a very good talking to when I get home," Ma said. She then stood up, shook their hands, and left.

When Ma was finished telling me everything that happened, I looked over at Aunt Marie. She had her face in her hands and wasn't speaking.

"Gary, my embarrassment aside, let's start off with the forgery. It is illegal to forge someone's name. Do you understand that? First and foremost, I want your word that you will never do that again," she said staring at me and waiting for a response.

"I swear, Ma, never again," I answered.

"Now, Gary, why did you write those obscene poems? You are a good writer I'm told. Why those?"

I just sat there.

"Gary, answer me," she said.

"I think I'm an okay writer, Ma. But I'm not a poet. I'm not good at that. So, I got the poems from someone else and just submitted them."

"Where did you get them, Gary? I want to talk to that person too about writing that kind of stuff," she said with her voice raising.

Again, I just sat there.

"Gary, answer me!! Was it Kyle?"

"NO," I offered.

"Was it Mitch?" she asked.

"NO," I said.

At this point Aunt Marie took her face out of her hands and said "Oh, please. Carole, this has Billy written all over it."

I just sat there.

"GARY, WAS IT BILLY?" she was pissed now.

"No, Ma it wasn't Billy" I said.

I'd never seen Ma so aggravated, she wanted me to tell her who it was.

She leaned into me and said, "Gary, who is the horses' ass that gave you those poems?"

I knew I was cornered. I raised my head, looked into her eyes and said, "DAD."

Aunt Marie put her face back in her hands.

Ma sat back and didn't speak for a few minutes. Then she got up, reached into her purse, slid a buck across the table and said, "go to the store, and get me a loaf of bread."

That was it.

I grabbed the buck and headed for the door. On my way out, I could hear them both laughing.

Ma never did mention it to Dad as far as I could tell because he was never pissed I ratted on him.

I told Mary I was gonna lay off of the shenanigans for a while when I was filling her in on the whole story. I said it very seriously too. Kinda like I actually meant it.

The following is the story submitted by Gary Simpson for the Halloween Edition of the school newspaper.

RETRIBUTION

PART 1

We were sick of the abuse. Tired of getting stomped on, kicked, beaten, and attacked. We were treated with such hatred and disdain. We weren't going to stand for it anymore. Our day of reckoning was upon us. We were going to take our revenge to the next level.

We will admit, we aren't easy to live with. We are hoarders and takers and scavengers, but we don't deserve the treatment we've received.

Aren't you the same if you think about it? Don't you do what we do? Covet and take what you want—when you want it? We are no different, really. Maybe that is why you hate us so much. No matter now, I suppose. The decision was made. The

King made the call, and the troops will follow. The army will obey.

When the time is right, we will strike. The plan seems flawless. We will climb the vertical black tower. We will find our entrance through the snow-colored mountains and execute our plan. We will feast there. The trip will be tiresome, but we will leave with an abundance of food to last us quite some time.

Possibly, one day another battle will be necessary. We will attack again if we must. It could be avoided should the next antagonist decide to just leave us be, but that is doubtful. They never do. However, a battle of this scale, the one we are preparing for tonight, is something we can only do when we've been pushed too far. The King has told us, to do so more often than not, would be a mistake for a number of reasons. Nonetheless, tonight we go into battle and take what we need.

As planned, we waited for darkness and quiet. In a calculated manner, we scaled the great vertical black tower.

The King found our entrance, and we followed.

There were thousands of us, as was necessary. The first few thousands had to immediately flood the open cave. Into it they poured, blocking anything inside from escaping. Flooded and packed, this kept things quiet. The next army of thousands found the food source, which was plentiful and started to rapidly feast. The law stated they feast for five moments or so, fill their pouches with food and head back to the fort. The next batch of thousands did the same until the food source was dry.

At the end of the battle, we were all hunkered down safely in our fort, full, exhausted, and already packing our food away for future need. This was a productive battle. We had accomplished every goal our King had given us, and he was happy. Now, we could sleep in peace knowing that we wouldn't be abused or bothered. We knew one day, it would happen again—it always does—but for now, there was peace.

PART 2

It had been a week since Mrs. Sinclair had heard from her daughter, and she was worried. Having moved to Florida last winter, her daughter promised to call her every week to check on her. Her daughter, Allison, wasn't ready for the Florida life and wanted to stay in New England. Lowell, Massachusetts, to be exact. She wasn't ready to give up the seasons or the city.

Mrs. Sinclair explained all of this to the police and asked them to just do a wellness check on her.

The police arrived at the house on West Third Street at 9 a.m. after the mother's call. When they arrived, they noticed there was a car parked in the driveway fitting the description the old women had given of her daughter's car. They had instructions to break into the house if necessary if her car was there. At this point, the mother just wanted answers.

Sgt. Mitchell and Patrolmen Cook grabbed the battering ram from the back of the patrol car, and within one minute they were in the house.

"Allison Sinclair, Lowell PD. Ma'am, please identify yourself," Sgt. Mitchell yelled out.

There was no response.

They began to walk through the house. "Nothing in the kitchen, sir," shouted Officer Cook.

"Living room is clear," shouted Sgt. Mitchell in reply. "You check the cellar and I'll head upstairs."

Officer Cook headed downstairs. It was an old house with an old, musty, damp cellar. It smelled of paint thinner and oil, and so far, nothing seemed out of the ordinary.

While he was down there poking around, his walkie talkie went off, "COOK, GET UP HERE NOW! FIRST BEDROOM ON THE LEFT."

Cook took two steps at a time out of the cellar and then ran upstairs to the first bedroom.

Sgt. Mitchell stood staring at the bed in disbelief. He had pulled back the sheet. On the blood-soaked bed, lay the skeletal remains, of what he assumed, was Allison Sinclair. Her skull still had hair, but almost all the flesh was gone. Her body had been cleaned dry of flesh right down to bone.

"What in the FUCK happened to her! I mean HOW?! WHY? Sarge, I don't even know what to make of this," Cook said with a quivering voice.

"We will have to leave that up to the medical examiner, Cook. In the meantime, let's rope the place off as some sort of crime scene and make the call," Mitchell replied.

As they were starting to leave, Cook stopped in his tracks and said, "Sarge, I'm gonna be sick. A few cockroaches just crawled out of her mouth. I mean, they were right in her mouth!" Cook started to gag and ran out of the room. Sarge followed.

As they were leaving the room, the last two members of the troop, whom the King had sent out to make one last check on the food source, made their way back to the fort. Their work was completed. There was nothing left.

CHRISTMAS MIRACLE

Ma was traditional. She'd decorate for every holiday. On St. Pat's Day, we'd have green shamrocks everywhere. On the Fourth of July, she'd decorate everything in red, white, and blue inside the house, and she'd make sure Dad hung a flag outside. On Valentine's Day, she put hearts in every window. A holiday wouldn't go by without being remembered. Christmas though… That was something else.

We didn't have much extra, but it didn't matter. We would pull out the four boxes of decorations she stored in the cellar and everything in them would go up. She kept the paper garland me and my brothers all made her with our first-grade teachers. Every year we added more to the garland, and now she had enough to circle the entire living room.

We had a manger of removeable plastic figures that each of us played with. We'd usually have Mary, Joseph, and Baby Jesus battle against the donkey, the cow, and the goat. This would keep us busy for hours. Ma always told us it was okay to play, but to let Baby Jesus win every time since it was his birthday after all.

Food played a part on the holidays, too. In our house, Thanksgiving was the only time all year we'd eat turkey and Christmas was the only time we'd get a roast beef. I looked forward to that all year. There was no calling the fat on this piece of beautiful beef. We'd have mashed potatoes, gravy, and all the fixings. We looked forward to the feast.

Another thing Ma made was Jell-O. On Thanksgiving, she'd make yellow and orange Jell-O, and on Christmas, she would make red and green. She'd layer it in small plastic cups and we'd pile Cool-Whip on top. We'd always grab for this before pie or anything else she'd make.

On Christmas Eve, we'd usually have Aunt Marie, Uncle Ronnie, Cousin Billy, and his two sisters, Maggie and Beth over. Mitch and his family would come, too, with their projector and Looney Tunes cartoons for us all to watch.

The Martin's, next door, would always stop by with Angie and Mary. Every year was the same, Mitch would try to get one of Billy's sisters under the mistletoe, but neither of them were interested in any of the guys we hung out with. They were both pretty girls and a few years older than us and thought all of our friends were morons.

When everyone would leave, Ma and Dad would send us to bed where we would lay in wait. A little after midnight, we'd hear Dad dramatically yell out the door, "SO LONG, SANTA! THANKS FOR COMING. SEE YA NEXT YEAR!" Then, he'd yell for us to come downstairs, and we'd get to open all of our gifts.

I found out later this was for two reasons. First, Ma hated surprises. She couldn't keep them and was too excited to wait until morning. Second, Dad was usually half in the bag after the Christmas Eve party, and he went along with Ma so he could sleep in a little later the next morning.

All of this stuff was great, but there is one Christmas that stands out in my mind more than any other.

It was two weeks before Christmas and I had turned twelve-years-old. I woke up early on a Saturday morning and went downstairs.

My folks were already out in the kitchen, and they didn't hear me come down. I sat on the couch out of view and read my new comic. To tell the truth, I was enjoying the alone time.

I heard Ma say, "Danny, what are we going to do? There are two weeks left until Christmas. We have no extra money—that new water heater took every single drop of our savings. We have no presents for the kids at all." I heard her sobbing.

After a few minutes, Dad said, "don't cry, love. We'll figure something out—we always do."

"I know, but this time I just don't see a way out of this. I may have to call the church," she said crying.

Dad did not want Ma to do that. Neither did she. They never wanted to accept money from the church or welfare or anywhere else. Ma used to say they were luckier than most homes in our neighborhood. We had two parents, and Dad worked three jobs. She'd say that money is for people worse off than we were.

"Give me a little time, honey. We'll figure it out," Dad said as he pushed his chair away from the table.

I snuck out of the room and crept back up the stairs. I knew they'd be upset if they knew I heard that.

The next few weeks, I walked around wondering what Christmas was gonna look like this year. I actually felt worse for my brothers and my folks. Aaron and Michael were littler and wouldn't understand why Santa couldn't make it this year. They still believed. But it would be worse for Ma and Dad not having anything to give us. I tried not to think about it as the next few weeks dragged on.

The night before the Christmas Eve party, I tried to cushion the blow by telling my brothers, "there are a lot of poor kids around this neighborhood, more than last year, who have no dads. Don't be sad if Santa has to bring them stuff this year and we don't get anything."

Aaron spun around, "DON'T GET ANYTHING—ARE YOU KIDDING ME!? I'VE BEEN TRYING TO BE GOOD THIS WHOLE WEEK!" he said with watery eyes.

"I'm not saying it'll happen, but just in case. Remember: We get a vacation to the mountains every year. I'm just saying— you never know. If the elves can't make enough presents, Santa will give it to whoever needs it more," I said trying to calm Aaron down a little.

Michael said nervously, "let's not talk about this guys. It'll be okay." I welcomed his optimism.

Our Christmas Eve party happened as planned with our usual guest. I kept looking at Ma and Dad for any sign of worry, but they were acting normal. They seemed like they were in good moods and having a great time. I had no idea what to expect.

As the night went on, the champagne and beer were flowing, and the grownups were all getting loose. Billy kept sneaking the last remnants of beer left in cans. The kids were all having a great time playing games, and I actually got a quick kiss from Mary under the mistletoe. It turned out to be a pretty good night.

As everyone filed out and we said our good-nights, Dad instructed us to grab a few garbage bags and do a quick pickup to help out. After bringing out the last bag, I heard Dad shout from the front room, "okay, guys. Head up to bed now—get going."

My brothers ran up the stairs without saying good night. I walked over to Ma; I felt my heart in my throat thinking of what she must be going through. I just grabbed her and hugged her, "I love ya Ma," I said as I held on tight for a moment.

She pulled back and looked at me with teary eyes, "well, I love you, too, Love. Merry Christmas. Off to bed now."

When I got into the room, my brothers were already in their beds. I stripped down, threw on my sweats, and crawled into bed.

My mind was racing. I felt nauseous and sweaty. I wanted to say something to my brothers because I knew they were laying there, waiting. I didn't think we'd be called down.

Just as I was about to open my mouth, we heard Dad! "THANKS FOR COMING SANTA! SEE YA NEXT YEAR!"

My brothers sat up in their beds, "I knew he'd come! He knew I was good!" Aaron said.

"I told you everything would be okay!" Michael announced while jumping down from the top bunk.

"OKAY, GUYS! HE'S GONE. COME ON DOWN!"

Dad barely got the words out when my brothers were already descending the stairs. I followed after them.

I couldn't believe my eyes! There were a bunch of presents under the tree. I could see all the big stuff first: Aaron had a cool giant blow up Pan Am airplane, Michael had a Louisville Slugger and a glove, and I had a four-person toboggan.

Ma and Dad were smiling bigger than I've seen in a long time. I was confused. I knew Dad wouldn't be as happy if they had to borrow or get help to get this stuff. I couldn't figure out how they pulled this off.

I'd find out a few days after Christmas.

My brothers were upstairs playing, and Dad was working his shift at the nursing home washing floors. Ma was in her rocking chair knitting and having a cup of tea. I sat in Dad's chair.

63

"Ma, I have to ask you something, and I have a confession to make," I started.

Ma's hands stopped knitting. She looked at me and said, "oh, Gary, what did you do now?"

"No, Ma. It's what did YOU do?" I countered. I confessed that I had heard her and Dad talking about having no money for Christmas. I told her how I had heard her crying and saying they didn't know what they were going to do. I asked her how she pulled it off.

She sat there a few minutes deciding if she should tell me. So, I offered, "Ma, I won't tell the guys. I never told them I heard you and Dad talking, but I was worried. Can't you tell me what happened?"

She smiled and the story went like this.

After her and Dad had the conversation, she laid in bed the next two nights praying. That Monday, Dad went to work at his full-time job. The owner called all ten employees in for a meeting to tell them that their boss had been fired.

He had been stealing from the company. He told them, in addition to the money he'd been taking for the last few years, he'd also been hoarding all of the bonus and weekly green stamps that the company had given him and told him to distribute to employees. They found all of the green stamps when they cleared out his desk.

Ma said the owner gave the merchandize books to all ten of the employees and said they had one night to use all of their stamps and pick out the stuff they wanted to get the merchandize in time for Christmas.

She said that night, her and Dad stayed up until 3 a.m. licking and sticking all the green stamps and picking out Christmas presents for all of us. Dad brought all the stuff home on December 23, just in time for Christmas Eve.

Ma laughed and said, "I still have paper cuts from all the quick wrapping we had to do that night." She held up her finger with a bandage still on it.

I sat there quietly for a minute while I was thinking about everything she had just told me. I finally broke the silence and said, "kinda like a last-minute miracle, huh, Ma?" She just smiled and nodded. I went on, "Ma, I gotta ask ya something though. Why anytime anyone asks you if you still believe in Santa, do you always say yes when we almost had no Christmas at all this year?"

She smiled and said, "it's because I do believe. I couldn't get through Christmas without him, Gary. He always finds us."

"Who knows," I sat there thinking, "maybe there really is a Santa."

STREET JUSTICE

One Saturday morning, I came down from my bedroom and stood at the front screen door. Michael and John were sitting out on the front steps and didn't hear me behind them.

"I don't know, man. Ronnie used to be an okay guy, but now he's a freaking asshole," Michael told John.

I knew who he was talking about. I *always* thought Ronnie was an asshole. He was a big kid who always bullied the little kids. He kept out of my way though. I guess it was obvious to him I could kick his ass.

"Did you hear what he did to little Petey the other day?" Michael asked.

"No, what did he do?" John responded.

"The other day, Petey was playing in his front yard with his two little buddies. They found a toad in his mother's tulips. They were all excited about it. Ronnie was on his porch and walked into the middle of the street and called Petey over to show him the toad. When Petey did, Ronnie said he wanted to hold it for a minute. He took it from him, threw it on the ground, and stomped on it. Smashed and killed it right there," Mike said.

"That's friggin' twisted," John shot back.

"That's not all–Petey started to cry, and then Ronnie pants'd him right in the middle of the street in front of his friends and anyone else who was around. Pulled his pants and underwear right down. The poor little guy started bawling harder, and Ronnie walked away laughing. I went over and helped him pull up his pants when Ronnie went inside. But I'll tell ya, John, if I had a few years on me, I'd have kicked Ronnie's ass right then and there."

"That sucks. The poor little guy—he's only about five. He must have been embarrassed," John said while shaking his head.

Just then, my eavesdropping was interrupted by Dad yelling from the kitchen that Billy was on the phone for me.

I grabbed the phone and started walking outside to sit on the back porch to talk to Billy. Last year, Ma had a twenty-foot cord put on the phone because she was sick of us stretching out the smaller cord.

"I just heard Michael and John talking about some fucked up shit Ronnie did to little Petey the other day," I filled Billy in.

Just as I was finishing giving Billy the details, I overheard Uncle Sammy talking loudly to Dad through the back screen door.

"Danny, I got a problem I gotta talk to you about. It's important," Uncle Sammy sounded urgent.

"Okay, okay. Sit down. What's this all about?" Dad said.

I told Billy to stop talking—something was up. I sat on the back porch with the receiver in my hand and listened. I could hear them talking from the T.V. room.

"Where's Carole?" Sammy asked.

"Out visiting Marie. What the hell is going on?" Dad said, forgetting I was within earshot.

"This morning, Millie told me that two weeks ago when Ann was walking to school some creepy guy pulled up and said something obscene to her. It happened three more times since then. One time, he pulled out his dick. This time, Millie was hiding at the top of the street where the bastard would usually come by, and got his plate number. Millie called the police."

Uncle Sammy continued, "they were afraid to tell me. They didn't know how I'd react. Well, it all came out this morning. I'm sitting there with them after breakfast and there's a knock on the door. It's the cops. I ask them to come in and asked

69

what this was all about. That's when I got the whole story. It seems they ran the plate and were coming over to tell us the guy's name," Sam said.

Dad interrupted, "did they arrest the son of a bitch?"

"Well, that's the problem, Danny. We know this guy from the Club. Don Winters. The cop said there isn't much they can do 'cause they didn't see anything, and Millie doesn't want Ann to have to see him again. She was traumatized enough already. So, without Ann pointing the finger at him, they don't have much."

"I can't let this go, Danny," he continued. "I mean I can't let this prick walk around like he got away with it. What will he do next? SHE'S A LITTLE GIRL, FOR CHRIST'S SAKE," Uncle Sammy yelled this and pounded his fist on the arm of the chair.

I'd never heard him so mad.

"Calm down, Sam. Calm down. Let me think," Dad said.

After a few minutes of quiet, Dad said, "doesn't Don's wife, Sandra, go to bingo with Carole, Millie, and Marie on Tuesday nights?"

"Yeah. What's bingo got to do with this?" Uncle Sammy asked aggravated.

"Hold on. So, he'll probably be heading down to the club for a drink while she's at bingo, right? That's when we usually see him down there: Tuesday nights," Dad offered.

"Yeah, he probably will. So, what are you thinking? Maybe we can pay him a little visit outside when he's on his way out?" Sam asked.

"Exactly. We'll have a talk with him. Make sure he understands we know it's him and what happens to sick motherfuckers who prey on innocent little girls. A little street justice," Dad said.

They were quiet for a minute and then Dad added, "Sam, I need you to just wait a few more days. Keep this all to yourself. We will take care of this."

"It won't be easy, but I will," Uncle Sam said.

"Hey, I was gonna take a ride to the packie. I'm out of Schlitz. Do you want a ride home? I can drop you on my way," Dad offered.

"Sure, and thanks, Danny. You are a good brother," Uncle Sam said.

"She's my niece, Sam. I have no choice," Dad told him.

71

I waited until I heard the front screen door close before I got up and told Billy we'd talk later.

Tuesday came, and like usual, Dad told me to keep an eye on my brothers. He said Ma was at bingo, and he was just going for a drink. He'd be back in a little while.

That was it.

He came home about three hours later and seemed fine. Like usual, Ma came home at 10 when bingo ended.

The following Tuesday was the same thing.

Then came Saturday. I was sitting on the couch watching *Creature Double Feature* — "Godzilla" to be exact—when Ma walked into the kitchen after getting off of the phone.

"That's odd!" she said getting Dad's attention.

"Marie just told me that Sandra and Don Winters packed up and moved away. We wondered why she wasn't at bingo last week. Marie called her and said Sandra told her Don was insisting on leaving. He came home a few weeks ago all beat up and just said they were moving and that's it. Not up for discussion. I wonder what was going on?" Ma asked.

Dad was quiet for a minute then offered, "Well, Carole, it's really none of our business. Don't you and Marie go concerning yourself."

"I suppose you are right," Ma said as she walked off.

I got up and called Billy to go for a walk.

A few minutes later, we were walking around the neighborhood while I was filling him in on the whole story.

"Geez, Gar. Sounds like they messed him up good. Well, serves him right! The son of a bitch had it coming," Billy said.

Just as I was finishing up the details, I looked over and noticed Ronnie sitting on his front steps.

"Hey, Ronnie, come here. I want to show you something," I yelled over.

"Yeah, sure. What's up?" he asked as he met me in the middle of the street.

I took a few seconds to look at him, and then glanced over at Billy. Billy looked at me like he'd seen this look before, and he took two steps back.

"Hey, is that a frog on your foot?" I asked.

When Ronnie looked down, I took my foot and stomped as hard as I could with all my might on his foot. He howled and bent forward. When he stood back up, I pants'd him. Right there in the middle of the street, he was bare-assed and balls out.

I grabbed him under one arm, and Billy stepped forward and grabbed him under the other. Together we dragged him up the street towards Main Street where there was a line of traffic. He was hollering for us to put him down and let him pull up his pants.

We dropped him at the top, in full view of everyone. I leaned forward, grabbed his face and said, "how do you like it? That's for Petey. Think twice next time."

We walked on down Main Street towards the sub shop like nothing had happened. After a few minutes of silence, I said "sometimes you just gotta take care of things yourself."

Billy put his arm around my shoulder and said, "that you do, cuz. That you do! Who's buying the subs?"

"50/50, Billy. Everything is always 50/50."

No Holds Barred

One Sunday afternoon, Dad was having a beer and sitting on the back porch listening to the ball game.

"Go take a shit for yourself! You call that a hit?" he yelled at the radio.

I went out and sat next to him. "What's the score?"

"5-2. Our guys are playing lousy," he was annoyed.

"Hey, Dad, can I ask you a question? Why do you always tell everyone to go take a crap for themselves? You say it all the time."

Dad chuckled, "yeah, probably shouldn't say it. Your Ma gets mad. But maybe it's not as bad as it sounds."

Now, it was my turn to chuckle, "how can it not be as bad as it sounds?"

"Well, what if you haven't crapped in a long time? You'd be glad to go take a shit for yourself, right? Besides, it's actually saved my life a few times," he said.

"Saved your life! How in the heck did going to take a crap for yourself save your life?" This I had to hear.

"In the war, it saved me twice," he answered quietly.

"The Korean War that you were in?" I asked.

"Yup," Dad answered.

I perked up at this. Dad didn't discuss the war much to us.

"What happened?" I asked.

Dad was quiet for a few minutes then said, "well, the first time, I had just got back from patrol with my squad and we were in a bunker. I was talking to one of my good buddies–another soldier from Iowa. A good guy named, Ted. He was a paratrooper, like me. All of a sudden, I got the urge to go take a crap. I left and as soon as I got into the latrine, multiple mortar rounds hit our bunker. Killed Ted—poor guy—didn't even know what hit him. Wounded six others. Ted had just found out the week before that his wife had a son. His kid would never get to meet him. Guess it was just Ted's time."

I just sat there quietly and waited for Dad to continue talking.

"The other time, I was on a hill in the Iron Triangle. Outpost Harry to be exact. We were told to hold at all cost, no holds barred. Whatever it took. The Chinese wanted that hill and came in thinking it would be an easy win. It wasn't. They threw everything they had at us. But between the U.S. and the Greek troops working together, we held that hill until the Chinese were forced to retreat.

Some of us didn't make it out though.

This brings me to a night in the foxhole. Heavy mortar rounds came flying one after the other, and I had to crap again. I held it as long as I could. Finally, things started to die down for a few minutes, so I crawled out of the foxhole to go. Just when I was far enough away, a mortar round came in and hit my other two army brothers that were in the foxhole I'd just crawled out of. One of them lived, but the strike blew his legs right off. I never saw him again after we got him out of there. The other guy was killed instantly.

Dad stopped talking.

I sat there taking it all in. "Geez, Dad. After seeing all that stuff, how did you not end up all depressed? I mean, losing friends that way, and yet you seem okay. How does it not get you down?" I asked.

"It could have, I'm sure. But my mum wrote me a letter once, and she said something that stayed with me in my head. She told me: Anytime God doesn't take you—when he easily could have—it's because he has other plans for you. So, do right by him and find out what those plans are and follow them."

"So, Dad, do you think God has some plans for you?" I asked.

"Yup," he answered.

"What do you think they are?"

Dad put his arm around me, leaned into my face, looked right at me, and said, "I'm looking at one right now."

"Wow," I said.

Dad just smiled and said, "yup." And he took a sip of beer.

"Hey, Dad," I said, "I'm sure glad you went and took a shit for yourself."

Dad busted out laughing, rustled up my hair, and said, "Yeah. Me too, buddy. Me too."

C.Y.O.

Now that Mary and I were in high school, we were allowed to join the Catholic Youth Organization (C.Y.O.). Mary was very into it, and I thought it was okay. We got to go to the rectory drop-in center and watch T.V., play pool or ping pong, and just hang out with all the other kids.

It was something to do on a Wednesday, Friday or Saturday night. Our folks liked it 'cause they said it kept us out of trouble. It was also supervised, but there were ways around that, too. There were hidden nooks and crannies for one thing— places I could hide with Mary to try to steal a kiss.

Another part of being a member of the C.Y.O. was that they offered dances once a month—another place with dark corners.

You had to be a freshman to go.

One night, Mary had to babysit her sister, Angie, who was only in the sixth grade. Mary wanted to go to the dance. So, she waited for her parents to leave, and then she convinced Angie she would have a ball if she came with us.

"You can't wear that though," she told Angie while looking at the "Kid Dy-No-Mite" shirt she was wearing. Mary gave her one of her flowy shirts, put a lot of make up on her face, and stuffed tissue paper in her training bra to make her look older.

"There's no way this is going to work, Mary. It's ridiculous. She looks like a little kid with fake boobs and makeup," I said. Mary disagreed.

And good for us because she was right. It worked and we got Angie in.

I remember this night distinctly because soon after we got there, we pawned Angie off with a few of our friends, and told them to take turns dancing with her.

Me and Mary found a dark spot behind the piano that was against the wall for a little make out session. I was leaving no room for the Holy Ghost (if you get what I'm saying). Just as we were getting into it and making out hot and heavy, Angie ran around the corner upset.

"Take me home! That kid, Lou, you told to dance with me tried to grab my butt twice after I told him to knock it off!! I WANT TO GO HOME! NOW!" she hollered.

The chaperone heard her big mouth, and so the jig was up.

I made sure to sucker punch Lou in the gut, when we walked by him on our way out.

All the other C.Y.O. dances we went to (without Angie) were pretty good. I didn't mind going, but I was too cool to fast dance. Mary would usually do that with her friends, but she'd save every slow dance for me.

Usually while the girls were fast dancing, me and the guys would stand around shooting the shit.

"That's three girls tonight I asked to dance that said 'NO,'" Mitch bitched, "why do I bother?"

"Stop being a baby. You are setting the bar too high and asking girls who are way too pretty and out of your league. Ask someone shy, or one of the girls no one else will ask. You'll get a dance and make their night," I counseled.

Problem was: Even those girls said "no."

I forgot when I advised him that Mitch was nicknamed "Mouthy Mitch." He had a bad habit of saying whatever was on his mind. This usually ended up with him pissing people off. He'd say moronic things like: "WOW, I didn't realize your butt was so fat" or "I never saw a girl with that much hair on her lip. You have more than I do." Needless to say, Mitch wouldn't be slow dancing anytime soon.

81

The dances were still great though, and they always ended with "Stairway to Heaven." One last opportunity to kiss and press against the girl in our arms before the lights came on.

The C.Y.O. also had a variety show that they put on every year. It was a singing and dancing thing—usually Show Tunes stuff. Mary signed up right away for the chorus. I signed up for set design. No one was getting me out on that stage.

I've never admitted it to anyone, but the shows they put on were actually pretty good. I still remember some of the words to the songs we'd hear while they were practicing. Me and some of the guys back stage would make up dirty words in place of some of them.

We replaced a line from one song with, "rings on dinks and butts on hoes." Another song became, "it's a treat to beat your meat with your Mississippi pud." The funny thing was, a bunch of the chorus guys heard us and loved it so they'd sing it our way. They'd get yelled at for it and told to go to confession. They were okay, though. They never ratted and told that it was us who came up with it.

We also met a few older kids I liked through C.Y.O. Mary made friends with this one big guy, Charlie. He was a junior, and he was a funny smartass. Right up my alley. He used to make me laugh. Charlie and Mary were more like brother and sister with the way they'd argue sometimes. So, I wasn't jealous that they were friends. He was actually a pretty good dude.

Mary told me that one time he drove her home from school when I was home sick. They were gonna go get a burger at Rick's. As she was getting out of the car, he told her to get back in. She put up a fight, but he said, "GET BACK IN," loudly. So, she did.

He drove her to her house and said, "go inside and go to the bathroom."

Mary told me when she did, she noticed that she was having her period and there was a spot on the back of her pants. She washed up and quickly changed and came back out and they went back to Rick's. She said she just shyly told him, "thank you." And he said, "I have sisters." And that was it.

She knew from then on, even though he was a smartass and sometimes aggravated the crap out of her, he was a true friend and he had her back. That could have been something that could have made her life hell as a freshman if everyone had seen that.

I liked him for that, too.

We had to practice a lot for the shows. They'd cram it all in about two months of practice and the third month for the show.

One night after Saturday practice, we all went back to our friend Tammy's house. Tammy was one of Mary's friends from school. Her mum was young and divorced and usually out with her friends on Saturdays and would let Tammy have the run of the house.

On this one particular night, we had a brilliant idea. There was a liquor store on Main Street, and they'd deliver booze to your house by cab as long as an adult received it. Tammy had one girlfriend, Gloria, who was a good-looking chick but she looked older than we were. She wasn't though. We got the idea to put her in a bathrobe and put a towel on her head, like she was coming out of the shower and to go down and get the beer.

The driver pulled up to the curb and honked. Gloria went down with all the money we pooled and got the case of beer. He never even suspected she was only fifteen.

"Thanks, Hon," we heard her say while walking with the case back to the front door. She came in, handed the case of beer off to me, whipped off the towel and robe and yelled, "let's get this party started."

We'd just opened Pandora's box.

This would become a Saturday night ritual through most of high school. We'd all tell our parents we were going to Tammy's house to listen to music. We'd tell them her mum said it was okay. We weren't lying, technically. But the folks had no idea what was really going on.

After we'd all drink, we'd all be laying around in the one big front room, crammed on couches or on the floor. There would be some hot and heavy making out while we listened to whatever albums with slow songs we had so we could keep the mood going. The room would be lit by the beautiful glow of lava lamps.

Funny thing was though, it'd never be more than kissing. We didn't have any friends that were going further than that yet-- not that us guys weren't hoping for that every single second of our lives. But right then, it wasn't on the table.

Once, while crammed on the other end of the couch that Mary and I were on, my cousin, Billy, tried to cop a feel with a girl Nancy he was making out with.

We heard her say, "one more time, Billy, and I'm done!" After he apologized, they went back to making out.

Billy told us on the way home that night, "I don't know how much longer I can take that crap."

Mary piped up from behind, "as long as you want to kiss, Billy, you will just have to deal with it. You aren't a dog for God's sake."

"Even my dog is getting more action than I am, Mary," he said as he stormed off ahead before turning the corner onto his street.

Mary said, "geez, what a baby. I'm glad you don't get like that, Gary."

I had to bite my tongue on that one. She had no idea. I was sure my balls were still a nice shade of blue from our make out session.

On the nights we couldn't go to Tammy's, we'd all walk over to 1st Street to party there. We'd have to pay Frank with enough money for a pack of cigs and a six pack of beer for himself, to buy for us. We'd stuff the beers in our coats and head over.

As the night would go on, shenanigans ensued. When us guys would have to pee, we'd just face the woods and drain the vein. When the girls had to go though, Mary would make all the guys turn our heads and the girls would drop and squat while holding a tree on the hill.

Mary's friend, Cheryl, who was a hot shit and had an unmatched love for David Bowie, could always make me laugh. Once, she held on to a tree at the top of the hill, and as she was squatting, she lost her balance. She fell ass-over-head and rolled down the hill.

We all turned around when we heard her screaming, and all we could see was her white ass up in the air. The guys were all happy to help her up but Mary told us to stay there and the girls helped her. I still laugh thinking of her walking up the hill, buttoning her pants with a head full of leaves.

Didn't stop her though, she shook herself off, grabbed another beer, and went right back to partying.

Some nights, the cops would show up. They'd give us a talking to and confiscate all the beer. We didn't have cars, so they'd just tell us to leave and remind us how lucky we were that they weren't calling our parents.

Billy said under his breath one time, "and how lucky are you guys getting all that nice beer to have after your shift?"

The cop spun around and said, "WHO SAID THAT?" And we all took off running. He didn't chase us and I'm pretty sure I heard them all laughing as we ran away.

This was the game we played with them many times, but they never called our folks.

Another thing we got to do with the C.Y.O. was the yearly ski trips. The girls and boys were separated with chaperones in rooms between them.

Most of the time the girls would be jumping on their beds singing and dancing to music. The boys were usually trying to find a way to sneak alcohol or blow a little weed smoke out a window without getting caught.

We almost ruined any future ski trips our first year. They were very strict about having no parties and staying in our own rooms.

Charlie waited until midnight and called a few of our rooms. "Party in my room at the end of the hall. I'll give the signal when the coast is clear."

Mary called my room, "are you guys gonna risk it and run down there?"

"Of course," I answered. "Peek out the door and go for it when he gives the signal."

We all quietly opened our doors to peek out. After about five minutes, just when we were all starting to say forget it, Charlie came out into the hall. He had a giant pair of his white underwear and started to wave them like a flag. All of the boys from my room were the first to make a run for it.

Just as we almost made it to the door, Mr. Gray, the male chaperone, came out of his room and took off down the hall after us. He grabbed me and Billy by the back of our shirts. Without a word he pulled us down the hall and threw us into our room. He turned and yelled, "I will count to five and whoever isn't in their room with doors closed and locked when I'm done, your parents will get a phone call."

Everyone bolted back to their room. We didn't try that again.

This wouldn't be the last of our shenanigans on these trips, at the shows, or the dances. During our years at C.Y.O, we always seemed to push it just far enough to get "a talking to," but never so far as to have any of it cancelled.

I feel like the priest and chaperones set a bar for us of what they'd put up with, and then lowered it among themselves expecting we'd do a little worse! We never let them down.

Good times!

FOUND OUT

One Friday night on his way home from work, Uncle Sammy stopped by. He had done a job for Abbott's Farm, and they paid him in apples.

"Thought you could do something nice with these, Carole", he said as he barreled through the door with a bushel of apples in one arm and a six pack of Schlitz in the other. "Danny around?" he asked Ma.

I heard her respond that Dad was on the back porch with me. Sammy came outside and handed Dad a beer.

"Thanks for the apples, Sam. We'll all make out in that deal—Carole makes a mean apple pie!" Dad said.

"That's the reason I brought them here, Danny Boy," Sammy said with a laugh.

They started talking about the game this weekend, and I kept one ear focused inside on Ma. She was telling Aaron and Michael she needed their help tomorrow morning.

"I'm going to make a bunch of pies tomorrow. Aaron, you help me peel. Michael, you deliver to a few of the neighbors. And maybe I'll get you guys that whiffle ball set you've been asking for."

They knew Dad would make them do it anyway, and this sweetened the deal. Ma got no arguments from them. I was waiting for her to drag me into this so I could tell her I had plans with Mary, but she didn't.

The next morning, they were already peeling and assembling pies as I made my way out the door. Mary and I had twenty bucks each and were going shopping. The plan was to buy a pair of jeans for me from Morgan's, and a pair for her from Browns. Then we'd buy a loaded hot dog at Mill City Dog.

In order for a girl to get a good pair of jeans in the area, Mary said you had to go to Browns. The jeans were great and not as expensive as other stores, but the couple who owned Browns were something else. You had to endure Mr. Brown waiting for you at the door and immediately asking, "YOU GOT MONEY TO SPEND IN HERE?"

If the answer was "no," he'd say, "OUT!" And you never even made it past the threshold. If you said "yes," he'd watch you like a hawk, and hurry you along the whole time.

There wasn't much for guys in there, but what little they did have, the guys weren't allowed to try on anyway. You had to hope for the best. Good luck trying to take them back if they didn't fit—that wasn't even an option. Mitch tried once to return something, and got tossed out on his ear.

Only the girls were allowed to try things on. They had to do it on the second floor, in a big room under the watchful eye of Mrs. Brown.

"I hate having to try my pants on in front of her," Mary bitched on our walk over the bridge.

"Then why do it? Just take a chance and hope they'll fit, or you could go somewhere else," I said.

"Because I can't get the jeans I like anywhere else cheaper. She glares at us when we try them on to make sure no one is going to steal a pair. I mean, I'm in my underpants for cripes sakes! Where am I gonna hide them?" she said.

I quickly got a visual of Mary in her underpants and no longer cared about the jeans.

"When do you want to eat, Gary? Now or after?" Mary asked as we finished crossing the bridge.

"I wonder what color underpants she has on right now," I thought.

"Gary, are you listening? Don't you want a hotdog?"

"Don't YOU want a hotdog, Mary?" I responded in my best pervy voice.

She swatted me and called me gross. We decided to eat after shopping.

I bought my jeans first. It took me five minutes, twelve bucks on sale, and no drama. Mary's purchase went as planned.

Mr. Brown was waiting for us at the door.

I had to wait outside while Mary went in. She was out eleven minutes later with a new pair of jeans for ten bucks.

Next stop was our loaded hot dog, and then over to Record Emporium. Mary wanted a few new 45s to listen to later.

As we made our way back over the bridge, we decided to take what little money we had left and split a Milkshake at Birman's drugstore. We had an hour to kill before we met Billy at his job at Main Street Chicken. He'd usually hang with us on Saturdays. Mary didn't mind hanging out with Billy because he made her laugh sometimes.

Sometimes.

We sat at the counter, ordered our Chocolate milkshake, and waited. Mr. B (as he was called) was the local druggist, but he also made the best milkshakes in town. Everyone knew it.

He was a pretty great guy, too. I'd hear Ma and her friends talking about him and how he'd trudge up the hill to deliver medicine to sick people in a snowstorm. Sometimes he'd go out in the middle of the night if they were in a bad way. Dad would always say they don't make them like Mr. B anymore.

Frank told me he liked Mr. B, too. He said when he was thirteen and asked him for some "sheep skins" (his dads' words—Frank clarified he meant rubbers), Mr. B said, "Francis, I won't be giving you anything like that. But more importantly, I won't be telling your mother you asked me for them. Now, on your way, knucklehead."

Frank said he didn't give him any, but he was still a good guy 'cause he kept his word and didn't tell his mother.

He said Mr. B finally sold him some when he turned eighteen. He said it was kinda weird because he practically begged Frank to take them then.

There might have been a few reasons for that!

When we got to Main Street Chicken, I could see Billy through the window. He was facing us, and his Boss was talking to him with his back to us. Billy made eye contact with me over the boss's shoulder. I quickly turned around and mooned Billy. I could see him crack up laughing.

I heard his boss yell, "THIS ISN'T FUNNY MISTER, THIS ISN'T FUNNY!" he was getting reamed. Mary swatted at me while laughing as I pulled up my pants.

Billy came walking out and over to us, "Gary, you trying to get me fired? He's already pissed off enough at me. I used salt instead of sugar in the whole batch of iced tea today. A ton of customers bitched. You made me laugh, and he freaked out."

"Did he fire you?" Mary asked.

"Nah, he's a humongous dick, but he knows no one else will work for him. So, he's stuck with me," Billy laughed.

By the time we made it back to our street, it was almost 2 o'clock—game time. We could smell the apple pies as soon as we turned the corner.

I ran in the house to drop off my bag, and told Ma I'd be heading to Mary's to listen to records.

"I'll be at Aunt Marie's if you need me. Mike's gonna deliver pies soon. Don't eat any of the Martin's pies," she said to me and Billy, "there will be plenty here for you guys."

We didn't argue. Billy and I had more important things than pies on our minds at the moment.

The houses in my neighborhood were very close together. I mean, all that separated you from touching your neighbor's windowsill was a small, alley-sized, side yard. It was barely even wide enough to park a car in. You could see and hear everything that was going on next door on either side. Fights, laughter, conversations, and you could even see what they were watching on the T.V. next door. On more than a few occasions I heard Mrs. Martin yell through the window asking Ma, "Carole, what channel is that you are watching? That show looks good."

Anyway, this came in handy for what me and Billy were up to.

When we got to Mary's there was a note on the door from her folks. It said, "we took Angie to see your grandparents. Gary and Billy can come over, but no boys upstairs and no shenanigans. Call us if you need anything."

We had our usual Saturday routine and would hang out there, and we never busted up the house so they trusted us. (For now.)

We went inside, and sat in the T.V. room that was right across from the T.V. room at my house. We could see Dad all hunkered down and ready for the game with his tray table, a bowl of radish, salt, and a Schlitz.

Billy looked at me and said, "NOW."

Mary stood up and said, "I want no part of this, I'm going in my room to listen to records. When you two dopes are done holler up and let me know."

Every weekend like clockwork, Saturday and Sunday when Dad would be sitting to watch a game the phone would ring. It was an old lady, and she'd ask him to speak to Arthur.

In the beginning, my old man would try to reason with her nicely, "lady, there is no Arthur here. You have the wrong number."

That didn't last long. Now, that she was calling a number of times on both days, all niceness on Dad's part went out the window and was replaced with irritation. Now, he loses his shit and flips out at every call, "LADY, FOR CHRIST'S SAKE! HOW MANY TIMES DO I GOTTA FREAKING TELL YOU? THERE IS NO ARTHUR HERE. GET SOMEONE TO DIAL THE RIGHT NUMBER FOR YOU, LADY! AND DON'T CALL AGAIN," and he'd slam down the phone.

I could hear the phone ringing next door. Dad got up and picked up the phone, "LADY, THIS BETTER BE THE ONLY CALL I GET FROM YOU TODAY!" Then, he slammed down the phone.

He sat back in his chair and five minutes later the phone was ringing again. This time I asked for, "Arthur! Oh, please! Get me Arthur!"

Just as I was tormenting the old man, I looked to the doorway in Mary's house and Michael was standing there holding two pies.

I hung up the phone.

"Why are you calling Dad acting like that old lady that calls him all the time?" Mike asked.

Me and Billy sat there silent.

"Come on, you know she pisses him off. She's been calling all weekend for the last six months. What's going on?"

Me and Billy exchanged looks. Billy jumped up and grabbed the pies, and I grabbed Michael "you tell Dad you heard us doing this, and we will beat the shit out of you! Got it?"

"Big deal," Mike said. "So you faked you were that old lady? She still bugs the crap out of him."

Billy and I started laughing at that point.

Billy finally said, "Hey, numbnuts. WE are the old lady."

Mike looked at us for a minute. After putting it all together, he started laughing loudly with us.

All of sudden from across the alley, we heard Dad yell, "SHUT UP OVER THERE, PECKAHEADS! I'M TRYING TO WATCH THE GAME."

Just as he finished the phone rang. We all stood looking at each other as Dad jumped up—completely pissed off—grabbed the phone, and screamed (before the person on the other end could even say anything), "LADY, THERE IS NO FUCKING ARTHUR HERE! GO TAKE A BIG SHIT IN YOUR SUNDAY HAT." He slammed down the phone.

Later that night, Ma told Dad that her mother had tried to call her to come over for tea, but must have dialed a wrong number.

"She said some lunatic screamed at the top of his lungs and told her to take an S-H-I-T in her church hat."

Dad said nothing. I loved weekends.

ANGIE

My bedroom door was closed. I knew Mary wouldn't be home for a while. Her and Gary were out somewhere. Lately, nothing could keep the two of them apart. It was annoying.

Don't get me wrong, I like Gary. I mean, he saved my life last year, but some things about him pissed me off. We've had our moments. One time, I didn't talk to him for two months because he tricked me into seeing Kyle Cote's privates when they were all big and bloated and gross after he had his rupture surgery.

He sent me over there with "bag balm" to rub down his "leg." Only it wasn't his leg at all! That was the first time I ever saw a boy's stuff, and I had nightmares for a week. I still get pissed just thinking about it.

So, I want no part of boys. But….

If that's true, then way do I get tingly every time I look at my Andy Gibb poster? Why did I just lock myself in my room and grab my Mrs. Beasley doll so I could practice kissing?

Maybe kissing would be okay, but that's it!

I've played spin the bottle before, and I have kissed. With Kyle (pre-rupture). Before his rupture, I was actually a little sweet on him to be honest, but now I'm not. I can't look at his face without seeing his privates. But I have kissed before. I just don't think I'm that good at it.

Mary yelled at me once when we were playing spin the bottle down Lance's cellar with the older boys. Mitch had spun the bottle, and it landed on me. I kissed him but he tried to stick his tongue in my mouth, and I slapped him across the face! HARD.

"I'm not taking you down there to play again. I can't believe you did that!" Mary said indignantly as we were walking home.

"He stuck his tongue in my mouth! What was I supposed to do? It's rude!"

"It's not rude, Ang. It's called a French Kiss, and ya better get used to it 'cause all the boys do that!" she said.

"Why? We're not even French." I was confused.

"I don't know why. They just do and they like to do other things, too. Not that you have to—I mean, you probably shouldn't anyway. You only just turned twelve, but it's the way they are." Mary walked up next to me and put her arm around my shoulder. "Ang, save the slaps for the stuff below the neck, okay? Give them a break on the kissing."

"Okay," I said. "I'll try."

I haven't played spin the bottle since that time because I still have the problem of not knowing how to French Kiss.

It was hard to practice on Mrs. Beasley. Her glasses kept getting in the way, her polka dot dress was distracting, and her mouth didn't open. I was basically licking plastic lips.

My friend, Karen, who has two older brothers, knew way more than I did. She also had a pair of white go-go boots that I wanted, but my mother still wouldn't let me get.

"The hippies all wear them," Ma said

"No, they don't. The hippies are all bare foot. Nancy Sinatra wears them," I countered. Because Nancy was older than me by at least fifteen years, I lost that fight. For now.

Karen was my good close friend. We shared secrets and also sang really good to my records with hairbrushes in my big mirror. No one could do "You Light Up My Life" like we could with such feeling and emotion. We were even better than Debbie Boone was.

Anyway, back to the kissing. Karen told me to make my hand look like a puppet, "ya know, like that guy Señor Wences from the Ed Sullivan show did. Practice kissing that way," she said. "Just make sure you don't get caught though."

Her Aunt Agnes caught her once and told her mother that she thought there was something wrong with her. Karen heard her say, "it ain't right, Dolores. She was doing something weird to her hand—something sinister."

When Karen looked up the word sinister, she was pissed. "Fuck Aunt Agnes," she whispered. "She's probably never had a kiss in her life. The old bat."

"Well, either way, Karen, between Mrs. Beasley and my puppet hand, I gotta figure it out," I lamented.

"Maybe when we get enough practice in, we will get some guys in our grade to play spin the bottle. Maybe they are like us and don't know how to French Kiss yet, either." She was trying to cheer me up, and it did make sense. We're in the sixth grade, but Mitch and those guys are all in the eighth or ninth grade.

"Anyway, I'm not playing with the older guys anymore. Pinkie swear we do that. And pinkie swear we don't tell anyone about Mrs. Beasley or our hands," I said as I offered my bent pinkie to Karen.

"I swear," she said as we locked fingers and solemnly swore our oath.

Shortly after, Karen had to leave to help her brother with his paper route. He would pay her a buck a week just to deliver to one house. It was Old Lady Eleanor. He hated to deliver there because her house was all decorated in Liberace memorabilia. This was weird enough, but she'd also call you in to collect the money while she sat in her chair with her feet up. This would be okay except her little chihuahua dog would lick her bare feet the entire time. Karen's brother said it made him sick. Karen didn't mind doing it and was known to say "a buck's a buck."

After she left, I settled back in with Mrs. Beasley and my puppet hand.

Maybe it'd be easier if I pictured Mrs. Beasley with Andy Gibbs' face and a satin jacket instead of her polka dot dress.

I loved Andy. If we got married, he could make his brother, Barry, be his best man. Robin and Maurice would be ushers.

We could have everything monogrammed with A&A and get matching satin jackets. I'd have him sing "I Just Wanna Be Your Everything" to me on our honeymoon.

I mulled over all of this for a bit, looked at Mrs. Beasley, and leaned in. For now, Mrs. Beasley would have to do.

SLUMBER PARTY

Ma was standing at the kitchen sink doing dishes when I walked in. "Ma, you gotta give me some money to take Mike downtown and get him some new jeans."

"What's wrong with the jeans he has?" Ma asked.

"They aren't jeans, Ma. They're fake jeans, they're green. They're for little boys. He's in the eighth grade now," I argued.

"I just bought them, Gary. Money doesn't grow on trees, ya know!" Ma said.

"Well, pass them on to Aaron then. Besides, Aaron shouldn't be wearing the matching animal stuff anymore, either!"

"Now, what's wrong with his clothes?" she asked annoyed.

"Ma, animals are great for little boys, but bottom line, you're standing in the way of them getting girls. Mikes in the eighth grade. He's gotta dress the part. He needs a good pair of blue jeans. He has his eye on a girl, and I'm thinking his green jeans just won't cut it. I'll even take him myself if you can get me a little dough."

"Okay, I'll see if I can get you a some, but you'll have to wait until Saturday. Far be it from me to stand in the way of love," she said.

The following Saturday found Mike and I walking over the bridge. "Thanks for talking to Ma about new jeans," Mike said.

"So, who are you trying to impress anyway?"

"She's this new girl in my school—Ellie. She's really pretty, and she has long blonde hair and big blue eyes. She's going to Angie's slumber party tonight. Mrs. Martin said me and a few of the guys could come over for a while and listen to music and stuff downstairs with them," he said.

"Are you gonna try to kiss her?" I asked.

"I gotta get to know her first, Gary," he sounded peeved I asked.

Mike was a little shy, and he liked to think things through.

"Do you know anything about her yet?" I was curious.

"Just that she moved here from Pennsylvania with her folks over the summer. Her dad got a job here. I know she is

107

good at art and social studies, and that she likes steak and mashed potatoes," he offered.

I laughed, "well, Mike, it seems like you know a hell of a lot more about her than I've ever known about most of the girls I've kissed," I told him.

"Well, anyway, I want to look good so she doesn't like any of the other guys first," he said.

"You will brutha–don't worry." I knew with the right outfit he'd catch her eye.

Mike was able to get two new pairs of jeans with the money Ma gave us. I let him borrow one of my flannel shirts for the night. He looked great.

"It's in the bag," I told him.

At seven o'clock, I walked over next door with Mike, John, and Eric. I was gonna hang out with Mary while they had their party.

Mr. Martin finished the downstairs at their house. He made it into a couple of rooms. Mary and I were gonna take the room with the T.V. in it and watch the Saturday night lineup: the Mary Tyler Moore Show, Bob Newhart then the Carol Burnett show. I didn't mind watching anything as long as I was hanging out with my girl and had some snacks.

The others would all be in the next room having their party. Angie had sodas, snacks, and a bunch of records to play. She also had decked out the room in Christmas lights.

Mary and I got our snacks and settled in on the couch. I had a clear view into the next room. I had my arm around Mary with one eye on the T.V. and the other on the little dinkweeds. I'd decide which would be more entertaining.

The first hour of their party they played fast songs. Only the girls were dancing. The guys were all just standing on the other side of the room watching.

Finally, after a while, someone caught on and they started to play some slow songs. I sat there watching thinking maybe now this would get a little interesting.

I kept an eye on Mike. He stood there with his buddies while "Seasons in the Sun," "Sideshow," and then "Hello, It's Me" came on. Finally, when "Time in a Bottle" started, he got up the guts and walked over to who I assumed was Ellie. He was right—she was pretty. He looked nervous but happy while they were dancing.

Whenever any of them would stop slow dancing though, they would all go back to their neutral corners.

"Jesus," I whispered to Mary, "this is going nowhere."

I scanned the crowd and yelled out to Mike's friend, John, "hey, John, bring me and Mary another root beer would ya?"

When John handed me the bottles, I leaned in and said, "take this empty bottle and go back in there and suggest spin the bottle."

"Gee, I don't know, Gary," John was nervous.

"Don't be a baby. Do it–this party is starting to suck!" I said.

John walked back into the room. "Hey, guys, anyone interested in a little game of spin the bottle?"

At first no one said anything. Then, Angie and her friend, Karen, piped right up and said, "WE ARE." (They figured this would be a good opportunity to try out their new French Kissing skills they had talked about.)

As soon as Angie and Karen sat down, everyone else followed. I saw from the other room, and whispered to Mary, "maybe now this will get a little interesting."

With every spin of the bottle, I was hoping Mike would get Ellie. He got Angie a few times and a couple of the other girls in the circle, but never Ellie. His buddies John and Eric, both got her, and so did a few of the other guys. I could tell by the look on Mike's face that he wasn't happy about it.

Just as Carol Burnett was ending, Mr. Martin yelled from the top of the stairs, "okay, boys! Time to wrap it up now."

That ended the game, and everyone stood up to say their goodbyes. I got one last kiss from Mary. When we left the house, John and Eric were already running down the street. We were the last to leave. Mike walked next to me not talking. I could tell he was bummed out. As we were getting to the end of the driveway, Ellie came out to the porch. "Mike, do you have a second," she yelled.

Mike stopped and turned around. "Yeah, sure. What's up?"

She ran over to us, "well, ummm, well…" I could tell she was nervous, and so I turned around like I was looking at something else. She continued, "I just wanted to tell you that I was kind of bummed out that we didn't get each other during spin the bottle."

"Yeah, me too," Mike said.

We all just stood there. It was getting awkward. So, I kicked Mike's foot. He figured out what I was getting at, moved in, grabbed Ellie, and planted one right on her. When pushed, the kid had pretty good moves. It looked like a pretty decent kiss.

When they stopped kissing, I pretended to be invisible.

Mike said, "Hey, Ellie, wanna go out with me?"

"Sure. Where?" she answered.

Mike laughed, "no, around here that means wanna be my girl?"

"OH," Ellie said, "well, sure. I would like that."

They smiled at each other. Mike told her he'd get her number from Angie and call her tomorrow as she ran back inside.

I looked at Mike, "so your girl likes steak and mashed potatoes, huh?"

"Yeah," Mike answered.

"Well, don't invite her over for dinner on a Sunday. She can't be in on calling the fat from Dad's steak."

We both started laughing.

I put my arm around him and asked, "so, was it a good night, brutha?"

"The best," he answered. And we went inside.

Sometimes a guy just needs the right pair of jeans.

CROCODILE ROCKING

Mary called out to me from her kitchen window, "Gary, are you there?

"Yeah, what's up good looking?" I answered from ours.

"Ma and Dad are taking us to Wigman's Beach. Wanna come? They said Billy can come, too, if you want. Angie is bringing Donna. We leave in an hour."

"Sure, I'll call Billy," I answered back.

I was excited to go for a few reasons: It was something to do instead of hanging around here in the heat; and I got to see Mary in her bathing suit. Maybe I'd get to hold her in the water. Nothing between us but a few pieces of wet, thin fabric.

An hour later, Billy and I were sitting in the back seat with Mary in the middle. Angie and Donna were in the way back of the station wagon. They were reading a *Tiger Beat* magazine and ignored us the entire way.

When we got to the beach, which was on the shore of Wigman's Lake, Mrs. Martin put her stuff on one of the concrete picnic tables and laid out the rules.

"Okay, we have our grill for hotdogs, and I made potato salad and punch. Come back here if you are hungry later. I know some of you brought money to go to the snack hut, but if you go there, don't go alone. Sometimes older kids like to go hang out there. Remember there is safety in numbers. Lastly, no shenanigans," she looked at me and Billy when she said this. "Now, go have fun."

Angie and Donna took off down the beach and set up their own spot. Mary, Billy, and I found our beach spot and laid out our towels. Billy asked me to be in the middle. He said he didn't want other chicks seeing Mary in the middle thinking she might be his chick. He didn't want to ruin his shot with any girls around here.

Which, at the moment, didn't seem like it would be an issue anyway. There weren't that many other people here. It was still early in the day—we had the whole day ahead of us.

Mary pulled off her t-shirt and shorts, revealing her red, white, and blue bikini. (Good thing I was laying on my stomach.)

"That's the best-looking American flag I've ever seen," I said.

Laughing, she said, "wanna swim out to the floating dock and hang out for a while before we lay out?"

I looked out at the dock and noticed Angie and Donna were already on it with their backs to us.

"Sure, but let's scare the girls. I have an idea. You two go under the dock and wait for my signal to grab their feet, I will distract them," I said.

"What's the signal?" Billy asked.

"You will know it when I do it—I'll flip out," I said and ran to the water ahead of them.

I swam out in front of the girls, "hey, ladies. How's it shaking?"

"Oh, hey, Gary. Where are Billy and Mary?" Donna asked.

In my peripheral vision I could see them going under the dock.
"Oh, they didn't want to come in yet. The water is nice, huh?" I said making small talk.

"Yes, really nice." Angie answered, as I continued wading around.

Just as I went to say something, I jumped up a little in the water, "oh Geez! Something just brushed up against my foot."

"Probably just a fish or something," Angie said.

"Yeah, you're probably ri—OH, MAN!" I said as I pushed up hard and fast, "SOMETHING HAS ME!!! HELP!!! OH, GOD!!! HELP!!!" I screamed and started to thrash around, "I THINK IT'S A SHARK!!!"

"GARY! GRAB MY HAND," Angie screamed while pushing her hand out. Donna was yelling, "OH, MY GOD! JUST LIKE THE MOVIE!" It looked like she was going to start crying.

Just then, Billy and Mary grabbed the girls by their ankles from under the dock. They started to flip out, screaming, and both of them fell into the water.

As soon as they realized what we did, Angie started yelling, "YOU GUYS ARE A HELL OF A LOT OF JERKS! GROW UP AND STAY AWAY FROM US! WE HATE YOU!"

They both swam away from us all pissed off.

"What babies," Mary said while we laughed.

Billy quickly got distracted when he noticed a girl by herself swimming a few feet away. She looked about sixteen, with pretty red hair.

"Hey, how's it going?" he asked. She smiled at him so he started to swim over to her.

117

As soon as he was far enough away, I grabbed Mary and started spinning her around in the water. She was laughing, then I maneuvered us against the side of the dock away from the view of anyone on the beach.

"Come here, pretty girl," I said and started to kiss her. That was going pretty good too. She's a great kisser. She was snuggling into me when I got a boner.

"Gary!" she stopped kissing me.

"Just ignore it, Mary."

She put her hands on my chest and pushed me back. "Knock it off. Cool down," she said, "come back on the beach and lay out."

"Fine, lets swim back slow," I said. My plan was foiled again.

When we got back to our towels, we noticed that a guy was laying out on his towel about six feet from Mary's.

This guy was the hairiest son of a bitch I'd ever seen in my life. I mean, monkey hairy. He was bald on his head, but every other bit of him was covered in short, curly, pube-like, black hair. Lots of it. So much, that the banana sling of the yellow speedo he was wearing was busting at the seams. Not from dick, but from puffy hair. It looked like the front of his suit had cotton stuffed in it. He also wore four thick gold chains around his neck.

Mary looked at me, made an EWWWW face, and turned red.

We both stopped looking and started rubbing some baby oil on ourselves. After about ten minutes, I started getting bored (I could only lay out for so long). I looked over at hairy man.

He was standing up now and rubbing oil all over himself. You could tell this guy thought he was a stud. He turned his back to us and bent over at the waist to rub oil on one leg.

Mary had a new camera and the film developed in front of your eyes.

"Hey, Mar! Sit up real quick. I want to take a picture of you. You look gorgeous in the sun," I said.

Mary sat up and handed me the camera.

"Tilt your head to the right, Mary,"

She did.

I took the photo, and we sat there looking at the picture waiting for it to magically appear. After a few minutes, we started to see it coming into focus. When it finished, we could see Mary's pretty face with her head tilted to the side. Her head looked like it was resting right against the hairy ass cheek of the hairy man who was bent over with his legs spread.

Mary jumped up. "You are DEAD Gary!" She said as she chased me all over the beach. When she finally caught me, we fell in the sand, laughing.

"RIP IT UP, GARY! I MEAN IT," she said.

"I will—as soon as I show Billy," I promised.

"Where is he, anyway?" she asked.

"Who knows? Let's go get some crinkle fries and a few drinks in the snack hut."

As soon as we walked in to the snack hut, we saw where Billy had disappeared to. He was sharing some fries and a drink with the red head.

"Hey, guys! Over here," he called. "This is Colleen. She's from Watertown. She's up here staying with her aunt for a few weeks."

"We're Gary and Mary," Mary pointed at each of us.

We sat with the two of them and ordered some fries and lime rickey's. We were having a great time. They were both cracking up at the picture I took of Mary. After laughing at it for a few minutes, Mary made me throw it away.

Colleen was funny, and she thought Billy was a riot. They both seemed like they were really into each other.

We were having such a good time that we decided to hang out for a while longer. I got up and fed the jukebox a bunch of quarters.

After a while, Angie and Donna walked in. They saw us and sat at their own booth. We waved but they both turned away dramatically. They were still pissed.

"How long are they gonna stay pissed?" I asked Mary.

"Who knows? They are both so moody lately," she offered.

They put their order in and just sat there with pissed off looks.

Then, "Crocodile Rock" came on over the juke box. I looked at Billy and smiled. We both jumped up and started doing the twist. We were twisting all around the place like we owned it. Mary and Colleen were laughing out loud.

Mary knew I didn't usually dance at all, and found it really funny. We made our way over to Angie and Donna and stood in front of them twisting like crazy.

They sat there determined to stay pissed, but after a few minutes they started cracking up. "You guys are dinkweeds," Angie said through giggles.

I put my hand out to her. She looked at me a minute then jumped up and started to twist with me. Billy did the same to Donna. Mary took a few pictures of all of us dancing.

We spent the rest of the day hanging out and having a great time.

When it was time to go, Billy said goodbye to Colleen. They gave each other a kiss before we had to leave. Neither thought to ask the other for a phone number or last name. They never saw each other again.

For years later, whenever the subject of Wigman's Beach came up, Billy would look off in the distance and say, "ahhh, my sweet, Colleen. The one that got away."

AIN'T THAT A PEACH

One morning, I called Billy and asked if he wanted to come hang out with me and Mike. When he came over, Ma answered the door, "come on in, Billy. Give us a kiss! Gary's in the shower—he'll be out in a few minutes. I just made some cookies, Go, help yourself."

He walked out to the kitchen, grabbed a cookie, and sat at the kitchen table. "Can I grab some milk, Aunt Carole?" he yelled into the other room.

"Sure, you know where it is," she answered, and she went back to watching her soap opera.

Billy and Mike were sitting there, shooting the shit when, I opened the bathroom door and stood there in my underwear.

"Oh my God, guys! Something is wrong. Something is very wrong! I'm freaking out!" I said talking like I had a mouthful of marbles.

"What's wrong?" Mike asked.

I pointed down to my crotch, "look!" I said.

Their eyes scanned down and saw I had a HUGE bulge!

"What the hell is going on, Gary?" Bill asked.

"I don't know! I mean, yesterday I moved some bricks around, and I remember it hurt a little. Today, this happened. Maybe I have a rupture—like Kyle," I said seriously.

Just then, Ma walked into the room and asked what the commotion was. I pointed down to my crotch.

"Jesus, Mary, and Joseph! Gary, what happened?" she sounded frantic.

"I don't know, Ma. I was just telling the guys about it. I lifted something yesterday, and then this happened today. Can someone come take a look and let me know what you think?" I pleaded.

Billy and Mike looked at each other, and I could tell neither of them wanted it to be them.

Ma stepped forward, "let me see."

When she got close, I pulled out the front of my waist band as she leaned in. Then I reached into my underwear and pulled out two giant peaches, "now, ain't that a peach, Ma?"

We all busted out laughing. Except for Ma.

"Gary, don't ever do that to me again! You scared the crap out of me," she hollered.

I laughed and threw the peaches back into the bowl on the kitchen table.

"AND DON'T PUT THOSE DAMN PEACHES BACK IN THE BOWL! YOUR FATHER TAKES THEM FOR LUNCH EVERYDAY!" Ma grabbed them out and started to wash them at the sink.

"Well, they'd be the best damn peaches Dad ever had," I said.

"OUT!" she said, but I detected a slight laugh as she said it.

We hurried out of the kitchen—cracking up—and went to my bedroom.

"So, what do you guys wanna do today?" I asked.

After weighing our options, we decided to grab our homemade fishing poles and see if we could catch anything down at the river.

Sometimes we wouldn't catch anything, but other times we'd usually just snag a carp. Once, Mike got lucky and caught a bass. It was a good time even if we didn't catch anything. We'd grab snacks, hang out, and just shoot the shit.

We packed my duffle bag with a few cookies and some bologna sandwiches Ma made us, threw in some juice jugs, and headed out.

Ten minutes later, we were sitting on the edge of the Merrimack River casting out.

"So, Mike, ya getting any action from that cute little blonde girlfriend of yours?" Billy asked.

"Cut the crap, Billy. I'm not gonna talk about Ellie. Change the subject," Mike answered.

"Relax, relax. It's just guy talk," Billy said. "How 'bout you, Gary. Any new developments with Mary?"

"Like I always tell ya, Billy, even if there were I wouldn't tell you. The quickest way to get a girl to stop giving you anything is for you to have a big mouth and spread it around," I said.

"Can't fault me for asking," he said. "Don't you guys wanna know if I'm getting anything?'

We both looked at him and Mike said, "we didn't even know you were seeing anyone!"

"Well, I'm not. I haven't got shit, but I just wanted to know if you guys were wondering," he laughed.

A while later, after we'd finished our food and didn't catch anything, we decided it was time to pack it in and head home.

Just then, we heard someone cough off to our right. From where we were sitting, we could see under the bridge.

There was a person under there all wrapped up in a blanket.

I got up and walked over.

"Hey, man. You okay? Whatcha doing sleeping under here?" I asked.

The guy under the blanket turned quickly, startled and said, "don't fucking touch me. Leave me alone."

"I wasn't touching you. It's just weird seeing someone on the ground sleeping under here. I just wanted to make sure you were okay."

"Well, now, if I was okay, would I be sleeping on the ground under a bridge?" he asked sarcastically.

"Okay, smartass. Fine, I'll leave you alone," I said and walked back to the guys.

A few minutes later, the guy came out from under the bridge and started walking towards us. He looked to be about fifteen or sixteen. He was tall and skinny and had long brown hair.

"Sorry for being a smartass. I'm just really tired and hungry. Haven't eaten in two days. You guys got any food to spare?" he looked embarrassed to ask.

"Sorry, man. We just finished everything we had," Billy answered.

"Okay. Well, thanks anyway," he said.

I stepped toward him, "I'm Gary, this is Billy and Mike."

"I'm Manny," he offered.

"You really haven't eaten in two days?" I asked him.

"Nope."

"How long have you been down here?" Mike asked.

"About that long. I had nowhere else to go. I ended up here a few nights ago. My old man beat me for the last time. The fucking, lousy drunk. I finally hit him back, but then got my walking papers for doing it. Guess I should have thought that through a little better."

The guys and I just stood there for a minute. Finally, Billy looked at me, "I noticed that you guys had cookies and a lot of bologna left at home. Can we help Manny out?"

"Yeah, I guess we can," I looked at Manny, "why don't you follow us, and we'll sneak you out some food. We'll try to figure something out."

"Thanks, guys. I'd really appreciate it," Manny said.

Manny only had the clothes on his back and the blanket that he snatched from the line in his neighbor's yard when he left. The blanket was filthy now, and he didn't bother grabbing it.

As we made our way to our house, Manny filled us in on more information.

"Yeah, Dad is a real son of a bitch. I get why Ma left him. He used to beat her something awful, too, when she was here. She went back to New York. That's where she is from. Her mother lives there. She said she'd send for me when she got settled. But that was three months ago, and I haven't heard from her. Not sure what I'm gonna do now."

"Wow, my dad can drive me nuts sometimes, but he never hits us. That sucks, dude," I said.

When we got to the house, we went around the back. "Mike, stay out here with Manny. Show him where the hose is so

129

he can wash up a little." Looking at Manny I said, "if you need to piss or anything, you can go behind the bulkhead."

Billy and I quickly grabbed some bread, bologna and juices from the kitchen. Billy went to grab Manny two peaches, but I stopped him, "take two bananas instead, would ya? Not sure Ma cleaned those enough."

I stuck them in a duffle bag with a pair of pants, a t-shirt, and a pair of underwear. Billy looked at me and I said, "might be a little big on him, but at least they're clean."

"Yeah, poor bastard. One change of clothes and a little food won't last him long," Billy said.

When we got outside, Manny and Mike were standing off to the side of the yard. We handed Manny the bag. He opened it and without saying a word devoured one of the bananas, then the other in about three seconds.

"Man, these are good. Thanks" he said.

Poor kid was starving.

Mike said, "I have an idea. Since Manny doesn't know what to do or have anywhere to go, why don't we go see Father Casey at the rectory? Maybe he can help."

We all thought it was a great idea and took Manny over.

When we got there, Matilda, the housekeeper answered the door.

She brought us out to the kitchen where Father was having a cup of tea. We sat down and explained what was going on. He asked Manny a few questions about his mum, her name and where in New York she was from.

"Do you have some clean clothes, Manny?" he asked him.

Before he could answer, we told Father we'd packed some in the duffle bag. He turned to Matilda and told her to take Manny to the bathroom and let him take a shower.

When she came back, she stood in the doorway, "Father, the husband and I can take him in for a few nights while you try to sort this out for him. Now that Patrick has moved out, we've got plenty of room," Matilda offered.

Father smiled and nodded, then looked at us. "Okay, boys. I think we can manage from here."

"Thanks, Father. Please let us know how he makes out, okay? And tell him we said good luck."

He told us he would.

The following Sunday after mass, Father Casey shook my hand as I walked out the door with my brothers and my folks.

"Gary, I'm glad to be seeing you. I wanted to let you know, we were able to get in touch with Manny's mother. She was so relieved. She said she'd been trying to contact him for almost two months, but his father wasn't giving him the messages. She sent him a bus ticket and notified me last night that he'd arrived safely and is settling in."

"Thanks, Father. We're glad it all worked out. I'll let Billy know, too," I said.

When I got to the car, Ma and Dad asked me what that was all about, so I figured there was no harm in telling them.

Dad said, "you boys did a good thing. I'm proud of you guys."

"Thanks, Dad," I said.

He thought I was saying thanks for the compliment, but I wasn't. I was feeling really grateful for my old man.

Thank you, Dad, for that.

MARY

One beautiful, sunny Saturday in June, I walked into the kitchen and found Mum making eggs for us. Angie had already eaten her breakfast and had gone over to Donna's. Dad was working some weekend overtime at the Mill.

I startled Mum when I walked up to her and kissed her on the cheek.

"What's that for, Mary?" she asked with a smile.

"That's for always telling me to be nice to people because you never know when you may cross paths or what they are going through," I answered. "You basically saved my life yesterday!" I added.

She grabbed our plates and sat at the table with me. "Tell me what that is all about!" she said while putting ketchup on her eggs.

I started at the beginning.

Last June, Mum and Angie walked with me to the new Mill City High School where I'd be going to in September. Angie and her were going to poke around downtown while I was at orientation, and the plan was for me to meet them at the Five

& Dime counter in two hours for some crinkle fries and a root beer float when I got out.

When I entered the classroom we were told to gather at, we were split up into groups. Of course, I was in a group with ten other girls, and I didn't know anyone. Everyone except one other girl seemed to know someone. I would have said something to the other lone girl, but she looked like she was ready for a fight with her arms crossed in front of her chest. She had a look on her face like she'd kick the shit out of anyone who she even caught looking at her. I quickly turned away.

As we meandered through the halls, I realized how big this school was. It was sure to be a change from the small junior high Gary and I came from. A bunch of my girlfriends chose this school out of the two available as well, and it wouldn't be bad once we were all together. For now, I was solo.

Our tour guide, a senior named Michelle, was nice and friendly. The tour started at the science labs where there were a lot of microscopes and petri dishes. Then, we made our way to the math and accounting rooms. There were calculators that had paper rolls and pull handles on a big table. Next, Michelle brought us to the room where the school newspaper was produced. That looked like a cool room. It had printers and a film developing room. After we left there, she took us to the typing classroom next door.

I was excited for this class. The typewriters looked cool. So many of them in one place. She saw that we were all interested in them, and she stopped to point out a few things about them and answer our questions.

As we walked in the room, we noticed there was a group of boys in there, too. Their tour guide, another senior named Josh, walked them over to us when he saw Michelle explaining a few features of the typewriters.

"This is the cap key. You can make capital letters with this, and see, there are number keys too. This wheel is where you feed the paper through, and these two black things that hold the paper in place are called your rubbers."

A number of the boys started to laugh out loud.

"What's so funny about that?" Michelle asked them.

One smartass answered, "what are those black things called again?"

"Rubbers," she answered, all the boys started to laughed again.

"What's so funny about rubbers?" she asked annoyed. With that Josh said, "enough of that. Move on out, guys."

I was standing next to Michelle as Josh passed her and he whispered, "morons."

When we left the area and started heading down the hall towards the art rooms, I reached into my back pocket where I had a pack of gum. I pulled out a piece and noticed that the tough girl from earlier was standing next to me. I held a piece out to her without even thinking. She looked at the gum and then looked at me. She gave me a head nod while taking it.

We walked on.

Later, we went outside and walked across the street to the building outside that Michelle told us was called the Annex. As we entered, Michelle told us that this building housed the gym and locker rooms. She told us we would need to take a few notes down about the gym rules.

"Even though you will be told them again, I'll tell you a piece of advice, now. They enforce every rule in here. Mr. Chase and Miss Mink are strict teachers and coaches. Do yourself a favor and learn the rules before your first day. You will get along better with them."

Everyone attending orientation was told to bring a pen and paper for notes. I noticed that the girl I gave the gum to didn't have either.

I tore out a piece of paper and looked in my pocketbook and found an extra pencil. Without a word, I handed her the paper and pencil. And without a word she took it and gave me another head nod.

When we were done touring the gym, Michelle let us know we could go. As I left, the tough girl and I made eye contact again. This time I said, "see ya around."

She looked back at me, nodded her head, and said, "see ya."

When I finished telling Mum this story, she looked at me and said, "that's nice, Mary. How did that save your life yesterday though?"

"I'm getting to that."

So, three weeks ago, a rumor started spreading throughout our freshmen class. There was a very tough junior, Patty, who had a whole gang of tough friends. Apparently, her boyfriend, Roger, had confessed when confronted with undeniable evidence that he had cheated on her with a freshman girl. He refused to tell her who it was because he knew she had a wicked bad temper. I think Roger was just as afraid of Patty as everyone else was.

In retaliation, Patty told her friends, "fine, I'll just kick the shit out of every freshman girl I get my hands on until I find her."

Her plan was that she'd go after the brunettes the first week, the red heads the second week, and finally end with the blondes on the third week. That was this past week.

All of us were so scared. Especially because it was really happening. Shelly (a brunette), got the crap kicked out of her by them first. We heard Shelly actually got into a karate stance (and said, "back off Muthafucka's,") but it didn't work. Shelly was a tough girl in her own right, and we figured if she still got beat up, we were in big trouble.

We all tried to lay low by getting our books in the morning so we wouldn't have to be alone at our lockers in the hallway. And we went class to class quickly. We were trying to be as invisible as possible.

This brings me too yesterday.

I had gym and had to walk over to the Annex. I was by myself. I walked out the door and down the steps just as Patty and her crew turned the corner. I stopped for a second thinking if

I should turn around and run inside or run ahead and hope to make it to the Annex before they got me.

They made the decision for me. They ran up to me before I could do anything. Patty walked up to me and got right in my face. I could feel her breath, "hey, Blondie. Do you know Roger?"

"Roger, who?" I played completely ignorant.

"Roger, my boyfriend!" she asked through gritted teeth.

"I don't know anyone named Roger," I answered quietly.

"Well, I don't believe you. Maybe if I beat the shit out of you, you'll remember."

Patty stepped back a few steps, balled up her fist to punch me. When, just at that moment, I saw one of her crew poke her head around one of the other girls to look at me. Through my fear, I thought, "how do I know her?"

Then I remembered the girl from orientation who I had given the gum and pencil to.

She put her hand on Patty's shoulder and said, "hold up. It ain't her. She's cool."

Patty stopped, confused, and turned to look at her, "ya sure?" she asked.

"Ya, I'm sure. She's cool," the girl from orientation answered.

Patty turned back to me and then back to her crew and said, "let's go."

As they walked away, the girl from orientation looked at me and nodded her head at me. I nodded back and ran to the Annex.

"Mum, I haven't even seen that girl since orientation almost a year ago, but she remembered me. So, ya see, if you hadn't told me and I hadn't listened about being nice to people-- cause ya never know—I might be sitting here with a broken arm and a black eye," I said with a smile.

Mum put her hand on mine and smiled back, "I like that story, Mary."

Just then our moment was interrupted by Gary at his kitchen window yelling over, "Mary, come walk to the store with me, would ya? I gotta get something for Ma."

Mum stood up as I got up to leave. She grabbed my hand and squeezed it and said, "I'm glad you listened, too, love."

She had no idea!

UNCLE

Mary and I were sitting out on her steps early one Saturday morning watching my dad water the little patch of lawn we had in our front yard.

Dad had the front door open and was listening to Hank Williams on his 8-track player. We could tell that he couldn't hear it over the incessant barking coming from the Dalmatian that lived on the second floor of the tenement (the same tenement where the hot single chick with the big rack lived).

"SHUT THE HELL UP!" he yelled at the dog.

The hot chick came to the window and yelled back, "DON'T YELL AT HIM! HE CAN DO WHAT HE WANTS!"

To which Dad replied, "BLOW IT OUT YOUR ASS." The hot chick yelled back, "YOU'RE MEAN."

Just as Dad was about to yell another insult because he could never not have the last word, Ma appeared at the screen door and said, "Danny, knock it off."

"Knock it off? Ma, back me up!" Dad hollered.

"I will back you up when you are right. Now get in here and eat your breakfast." Dad threw down the hose and went inside.

Mary and I looked at each other and burst out laughing.

"He is some kind of nut sometimes," I said to her.

"Be nice, Gary," she said. "I always tell everyone how much you are just like your father."

I thought about this a minute and had no come back. I was a lot like the old man, but this wasn't necessarily a bad thing.

Changing the subject, Mary asked, "what did we want to do today?"

"I can't do anything. We have a big match planned," I told her. "We have the N.W.C."

The N.W.C. was the Neighborhood Wrestling Cooperation. Mary hated it. We formed it a year ago and had built up quite a neighborhood following. We got the idea after attending one of the infamous wrestling matches held at the Auditorium on Thursday nights with Dad and Uncle Sammy.

"When are you going to outgrow that, Gary? It's stupid and you know it's only a matter of time before someone really gets hurt."

"We have a great time, Mary. We charge 25 cents a show, and now we have a pretty good audience. Why don't you just come and watch?" I asked.

"Because I have—you know that—and I hate it," she shot back.

"Well, we are in too deep now. We have fans who want to see us. Especially now that we have stage names and stuff. We can't turn our backs now." I was hoping that would impress her, but it didn't. She just told me to call her when we were done "playing."

We had worked hard at putting it all together. We got a bunch of 2X4 pieces of leftover wood from Dad. And we had used some rope to make the ring. We used a big piece of painters' cloth for the floor. We also painted a wooden palette - green with red letters that spelled out "THE N.W.C."

Billy's character was COUNTRY BOY. He wore a pair of Michael's farmer jeans. They were too small for him, but they made him look bigger, which was the idea. His signature move was THE VICE.

I was STYMIE JOE WILCOX. I played the kind of guy you'd find working as a carnie—one who was tough and street smart. My outfit was a pair of jeans and no shirt. My signature move was THE KEISTER DROP, which was administered with a loud burp.

Michael was MIGHTY MIKE: The Boxer. He wore a pair of pale blue satin shorts with a white stripe down the side that Mary donated in the beginning when she didn't know too much about the N.W.C. He used boxing gloves he got for his birthday. Mighty Mike was known for his fancy foot work, and his signature move with THE ROUND UP PUNCH.

Aaron was PUNKY. He'd wear dirty clothes and mess up his face and hair with dirt and act crazy. He'd come running into the ring and climb up the palette we had in the back and make animal noises and breathe heavy. He was little, but he'd try to scare his opponents to make them think he was nuts. His signature move was THE CRAZY HEADBUTT. He'd hit you in the butt with his head and knock you down.

On the occasion that Jack, Mrs. Moran's grandson, was around, he would be our special guest. He was known as J BONE BREAKER. His signature move was THE J BREAKER. He wore a black t-shirt with a white bone that we painted on the front and fake brass knuckles that Mitch gave him from his spy kit. He was undefeated.

Mitch was the MC of the matches. He'd introduce us loudly and dramatically. He was a true showman. We'd all wait down in the cellar with the bulkhead opened and wait to be introduced. We wouldn't come out until it was our turn.

Angie was the money collector. We figured she was the most honest so we knew she wouldn't screw us. We gave her a cut at the end of the matches for collecting based on how many kids showed up.

We'd never fight each other in these matches. We'd invite members of the audience to enter the ring for a chance to claim the title. When I say chance, this meant anyone who "won" had to then defeat all the other wrestlers as well to become a member, which was pretty much impossible.

Jack was in town on this particular Saturday. We all met in the back yard to set up an hour before the match.

"This is gonna be a big one today, guys," Billy said. "We need to pull out all the stops and give the fans what they want. No holding back."

When the fans started to file into the side yard, we gave Mitch our sheet of paper with the lineup, and then we all went down into the cellar to get into costume.

Twenty minutes later we heard Mitch ring his bell.

"LADIES AND GENTLEMEN! WELCOME TO THE N.W.C MATCH ON THIS DAY, SATURDAY, JUNE 8. FIRST UP, WE HAVE STYMIE JOE WILCOX."

As soon as I heard my name, I downed my can of soda and ran up the stairs. I entered the ring and strutted around like the tough guy I was.

"LET'S GIVE STYMIE A BIG ROUND OF APPLAUSE!" Mitch yelled. When the applause died down, Mitch continued, "WHO IN THE AUDIENCE WOULD LIKE TO TRY TO CLAIM HIS TITLE?"

Because they knew Stymie was really me, and most of the kids in the neighborhood were afraid of me, no one immediately volunteered. Mitch kicked it up a notch.

"JUST THINK: WHOEVER DEFEATS STYMIE GETS THE CHANCE TO MOVE TO THE NEXT LEVEL AND TAKE HIS PLACE IN THE N.W.C. THEY'LL GET ALL THE PERKS AND BENEFITS OF BEING A MEMBER. AND THAT'S NOT TO MENTION BRAGGING RIGHTS, TOO."

With that, three hands shot up. Mitch picked Kyle. Kyle was pissed he wasn't asked to be a member to begin with, and he wanted to give it a shot and knock me off of my pedestal.

The match lasted ten seconds. As soon as Kyle entered the ring I waited for the bell and ran up to Kyle, lifted him in the air, and gave him the infamous Keister Drop followed by a loud burp right in his face. Kyle was down and the match was over.

Mitch held up my hand in victory and said, "STYMIE PULLS IT OUT! GREAT TRY BY KYLE. BETTER LUCK NEXT TIME."

"NEXT UP IS MIGHTY MIKE," Mitch yelled. Mike ran up the stairs shadowboxing invisible opponents as he made his way to the ring.

"WHO WILL BE NEXT TO TRY TO DEFEAT MIGHTY MIKE?"

Mitch had barely got the sentence out when Dave from two streets over shot his arm up into the air. Dave had been trying to defeat Mike for over a year and would take a pounding every time. We actually almost considered making him a member because of pure perseverance, but then we decided we liked the matches between him and Mighty Mike.

The match went the same as always with Mighty dancing around the ring. They'd both lay a few punches until it finally ended with Mighty doing the Round Up Punch that would knock Dave to his knees.

"OH, GOOD EFFORT BY DAVE! BUT MIGHTY MIKE TAKES HIM DOWN WITH HIS FAMOUS ROUND UP

149

PUNCH," Mitch yelled while holding up Mighty's hand. Dave walked out of the ring defeated.

"LADIES AND GENTLEMEN! NEXT, WE HAVE OUR SPECIAL GUEST! J BONE BREAKER!

Jack ran up the stairs and into the ring while breaking pretzel rods, like they were bones, and throwing them into the audience.

"WHO AMONG YOU IS BRAVE ENOUGH TO TAKE ON THIS UNDEFEATD CHAMPION?" Mitch yelled.

Ronnie, the chubby bully from the next street over, stood up and yelled, "I will, and I'll kick his ass, too!"

"OHHH, WE HAVE A CONTENDER. STEP RIGHT UP, RONNIE. SHOW US WHAT YOU'VE GOT."

None of us could stand Ronnie. I've had my run-ins with him and squashed him every time.

This ended up being the quickest match of the day.

When Ronnie entered the ring, Mitch told them to meet in the middle to shake hands. As soon the bell rang, J Bone got a hold of Ronnie's hand, and he bent his thumb all the way back to the inside of his wrist. It hurt him so much that Ronnie slid to his knees and yelled, "UNCLE!"

Mitch rang the bell and yelled, "NICE TRY, RONNIE, BUT NO CIGAR! J BONE BREAKER USES THE BONE THUMB BREAKER MOVE, AND HE KEEPS HIS RECORD AS UNDEFEATED."

Everyone in the audience clapped at little harder at this outcome.

"NEXT UP, FOLKS, WE HAVE PUNKY! BE CAREFUL AND STAY IN YOUR SEATS. PUNKY IS UNPREDICABLE!"

Punky started acting nuts before he got to the top of the stairs. He ran out of the cellar and jumped around like a gorilla and climbed on the palette while beating his chest. Then, he ran into the middle of the ring and howled like a wolf and then stood there panting.

"WHO HERE TODAY IS BRAVE ENOUGH TO FACE OFF WITH PUNKY?" Mitch asked.

Little Petey from the next street over was the only one to raise his hand. He was a little guy and only five-years-old.

"OKAY, FOLKS! WE HAVE THIS VERY BRAVE, LITTLE GUY. LET'S SEE HOW THIS GOES."

Mitch walked over to Punky and whispered to him, "easy on this one." When Petey got into the ring, they both started to run around in circles. Petey was laughing out loud, and you could tell that Punky was trying not to do the same. Finally, after five minutes of it going nowhere, Punky ran over to Petey, turned him around, and gave him a soft headbutt. Then, he gently lowered him to the mat.

"WELL, FOLKS, PUNKY WINS THAT MATCH, BUT THAT WAS PROBABLY THE BEST EFFORT OF THE DAY!

LET'S GIVE A ROUND OF APPLAUSE TO PUNKY AND
PETEY!"

Everyone clapped, and Petey stood there smiling. Mitch
helped him out of the ring while Punky ran around like a nut a
few more times before he came back downstairs.

"NOW, LADIES AND GENTLEMAN, IT IS TIME FOR
THE LAST MATCH OF THE DAY! PLEASE WELCOME
COUNTRY BOY!"

Billy ran up the stairs. He was in his signature overalls
with his messed up, bushy hair. He was also barefoot and chewed
on a piece of straw. He jumped into the ring and stared
menacingly into the audience.

"WHO IS BRAVE ENOUGH TO TAKE ON
COUNTRY BOY AND HIS INFAMOUS MOVE, THE VICE?"
Mitch yelled.

One hand shot up. Stanley from Main Street.

"WE HAVE A TAKER, FOLKS! PROCEED AT YOUR OWN RISK, STANLEY."

When he got into the ring, Mitch had them shake hands. Country Boy looked at Stanley and said, "you are going down, son!"

The first few minutes proved to be a pretty good match. Stanley was holding his own while they wrestled all around the mat. They each got a few licks in and more than a couple of body slams. Just when it looked like Stanley was about to win, Country Boy decided it was time for his signature move. He got behind Stanley, wrapped his arm around his neck, and took him down to the mat in a chokehold.

Stanley passed out right there on the mat.

He was out cold for a few seconds while Country Boy broke character in a panic.

Billy slapped Stanley's face and said, "Oh, shit! Oh, shit! Come on. Wake up!"

Everyone in the audience was on their feet. Angie, in a panic, ran into the house to get Ma. Angie was always a little bit of a fink.

A few seconds, that seemed like minutes, went by before Stanley woke up. He sat up dazed as Country Boy helped him to his feet.

Mary, who had been sitting on her back porch hearing everything, ran over to the yard. She ran into Ma who came outside with Angie.

"WELL, FOLKS, THAT WAS A CLOSE ONE! COUNTRY BOY TAKES THAT MATCH WITH HIS INFAMOUS MOVE, THE VICE. GOOD TRY THOUGH, STANLEY," Mitch yelled trying to pass everything off as good.

"OK, BOYS! THAT IS IT! THIS IS THE END OF THE WRESTLING CLUB. NO MORE MATCHES, *EVER*! AM I UNDERSTOOD?" Ma yelled in front of everyone.

"BUT, MA! COME ON—HE'S FINE!" I tried to argue.

Mary walked over to me gritting her teeth and said, "THIS PARTY IS OVER! IT'S OVER, GARY. OVER!" And she swept her hands through the air making it final.

Ma and Mary were pissed. We all knew we were licked. This was the end of The Neighborhood Wrestling Cooperation. It was our last match.

I looked at the guys. Then, I looked at Mary, hung my head, and said, "uncle".

DEBI

During the fall of '77, I began noticing that there was something different about Frank. Every time I saw him, the last few weeks anyway, he had pants on. He no longer wore only his boxers. He didn't seem to be smoking as much, either. One afternoon, as he made his way inside after work, I walked over to the fence.

"What's up with you?"

"What ya mean, dinkweed? I'm coming home from work. What's it look like?" he answered.

"I mean, something is different. Like, you wear your pants a lot now, and you haven't been out smoking as much."

He was quiet for a minute. Then, he looked at me with a serious face and said, "Debi."

I looked at him waiting for more.

"She's a new girl I met at work. She's more refined than I am. She lives up on The Hill—for Christ's sake."

When he said The Hill, I knew where he meant. The upper hill in town was a little richer than the bottom of the hill where we were. Our neighborhood had the stores, tenements, and

157

the busy main street. The Hill had more trees, and the houses were bigger and nicer. The Reservoir was up there, too. The Hill just seemed quieter.

A lot of the people who lived there probably had the same hardships as we did—I mean, it wasn't the richest section of town—but they just seemed like they had a few more white-collar folks. Store owners and such. Whereas at the bottom of The Hill, we had welders, maintenance workers and garbage men. These were all honorable jobs, but it just seemed a little different.

Frank said that Debi didn't smoke or swear as much as he did and that she wouldn't like him walking outside in his boxers. He didn't want to screw this one up as he said, "there's just something about her."

I'd soon find out what he meant.

The following Saturday, I hung out at Mitch's house. We were out in his back yard, and he was trying to show me how to light a fire like he learned in boy scouts.

The house next to his was the Booth's. They had two boys who were both bad news.

As we tried to light a fire, the younger brother, Ray, who was Michael's age, came out and stood at the fence. He yelled, "hey, asswipes. What are you doing, fuckheads?"

"Nothing that is any of your business–take off," Mitch answered.

"What did I tell you about talking to me like that?" Ray countered.

"Well, mind your own damn business and leave us alone," Mitch said. He was pissed.

With that, the little shit picked up a rock and lobbed it over at us. It bounced right off of Mitch's head and knocked him out.

Without even thinking, I jumped up, hopped the fence, and popped him one in the face. As he ran off, he told me to watch my back because he was gonna have his brother kick the shit out of me on the way home tonight.

I ran over to Mitch who was coming to and helped him into the house. As he sat there with a bag of ice on his head, his frantic mother called the doctor who told her what to watch for.

When I knew he was okay, I sat there for a while thinking about what I was going to do. I really was in no mood to get my ass handed to me. Truth be told, I knew the oldest Booth brother, Willie, could do it.

He'd hit first and ask questions later. I can't say I blamed him. I may have done the same for my brothers, too. But when it's you on the receiving end of a possible ass kicking—well, it's different.

I stalled leaving by telling Mitch's mother I'd sit with him for a bit while she made dinner to make sure he was okay.

I came up with a plan. There was only one person I knew I could call. When Frank answered the phone on the second ring, I said, "Listen, I need your help with something." I filled him in on what happened and he was quiet for a minute.

"I want to help you, but Debi is here. I don't know how she would feel about that."

I asked Frank to let me talk to her. Funny thing was, I knew he would let me talk to her. 'Cause for all the fuckery between us, at the end of the day, I always knew I could count on him.

He whispered, "you say anything you shouldn't, and it's me who will kick your ass."

Debi got on the phone, and I introduced myself in my best fake polite voice. I explained the situation. She was quiet, handed the phone to Frank, and I heard her say, "you have to."

"I'll be right there, dinkweed, be outside," Frank said before hanging up.

I was waiting for Frank at the fence when Willie showed up on the other side and said, "your ass is mine, fucker. You punched my brother in the face."

"Did he tell you why?" I asked.

"I don't care why. You punched him, and now I punch you back even harder and longer," he promised.

As he put his hand on the gate, Frank and Debi turned the corner. I could see right away what Frank saw in her. She had long blonde hair, a nice rack, and a pretty face.

She stood back while Frank approached.

Now, in a normal situation, Frank wouldn't have said a word to Willie. He would have gone right up to him, clocked him one, and that would have been the end of it. But this time he was more guarded. He knew what he had to do, but didn't want to look bad in front of Debi. He wanted to give the appearance of being the good guy.

He walked up to Willie and said, "so, you want to kick his ass, huh?"

Willie stumbled a bit, "well, what choice do I have Frank? He punched my brother in the face!"

"Okay, I hear that. I'd want to pop him, too, but your little shithead brother knocked Mitch out with a rock. Did he tell you that? Isn't there some friend code, too, you know about? If someone knocked your buddy out with a rock, wouldn't you need to kick his ass too?"

"Yeah, but…."

"Yeah, but!" Frank mocked. "So, here's what I say we do, Willie. Gary kicked your brother's ass for what he did to Mitch, right? Friend code. Now you are going to kick Gary's ass for kicking your brother's ass. Brother code—"

I don't like the sound of that one, I thought.

"—Then," Frank continued, "I'm going to kick the living shit out of you for kicking Gary's ass. Again, friend code."

Willie looked at Frank for a minute mulling over this outcome. Just like Willie knew he could easily kick my ass, he was no dummy, and knew Frank could kick his.

While they were both quiet for a minute, Debi stepped forward and said, "there is another way out of this, guys."

Everyone stopped to look at her.

"How about your younger brother goes and apologizes to Mitch? After all—Willie, is it?" Willie looked at her and nodded. She continued, "well, after all, Willie, your brother did start it. Then, when he apologizes to Mitch, Gary will apologize to him and then we will all just forget about this. How does that sound to everyone?"

Frank stood there with his arms folded starring at Willie. I felt like he was telepathically telling him that if he didn't agree, he would be a dead man.

After a few seconds that seemed like an hour with Willie thinking about this, he took a few steps back and said, "I guess that sounds okay. I'll go get Ray and make him apologize."

A few minutes later, we stood on Mitch's porch. Frank and Debi were there because I'm sure Frank wanted to make sure it all went off as discussed.

Willie walked over to Mitch holding Ray tightly by the arm, "OKAY, OKAY. FINE! I'm sorry," Ray said unconvincingly then he looked at Willie and said, "HAPPY?" Willie looked pissed at him.

I reluctantly walked over to Ray to apologize as agreed.

Willie put his hand up to stop me, "Don't apologize, Gary." He turned to Ray and said, "you deserved the punch. You started the whole thing, you little shit. Do it again, and I won't stand up for you." He grabbed Ray by the shirt and they left the porch.

The silence was broken when Debi looked at us and said, "see? I knew it'd all work out."

Frank smiled bigger than I've ever seen him smile before and said, "it's all because of you, my sweetheart," as he grabbed her hand.

Debi smiled back—she really had a beautiful smile—one that Frank would say later "that lit up a room."

As they walked home arm and arm in front of me, I thought, "Jesus, this guy is whipped!"

Frank was a changed man from then on. Don't get me wrong, after a few months of being with Debi, he let his guard down. Every once in a while, when she wasn't around, he'd come outside in his boxers to have a butt and tell us what a bunch of dinkweeds and morons we were. It just wasn't as often.

It wasn't as often, because Frank was in love.

This was a good thing, for all of us.

EPILOGUE

One night, years later, Mary sent me into Lowell to get some pizza for dinner. Living in the suburbs was great, but Lowell still had the best pizza.

After I picked it up, I decided to take a quick ride through the old neighborhood on my way home. I hadn't been back in years. Not since the time we took the boys for a little stroll down memory lane.

I pulled up in front of the old house, and a man, about thirty-years-old, came out and sat on the front steps. He looked over at me suspiciously and asked, "can I help ya with something?"

"Actually," I answered, "I grew up here. In this house."

"No shit?" he said sounding interested, "how long did you live here?"

Until 1985 when I married the girl next door. I see you kept Dad's roses going in the front yard. You still got the grape vine in the back?" I asked.

"Yeah, it's a good one too. I get a lot of grapes. Wanna take a look?" He started to stand up.

"Sure, if you don't mind."

I shut off the car and followed him out to the back through the side yard. Was this how small the yard really was? It seemed so much bigger growing up.

I guess living on an acre and a half now it would, I thought.

When we got to the back, I saw the grape vine Dad tended to for years. Ma used to make jelly with those grapes every season. We'd have so many grapes she'd give bags to old lady Moran so she could make wine and jelly of her own. Ma would tell her that it was the least she could do considering all the pears, rhubarb, and blackberries we feasted on in her yard over the years.

"I built her a nice arbor," he said while pointing it out to me, "that thing grows like a weed."

"Yeah, it used to when Dad took care of it, too. He'd train it with string to go around the porch." Just as I said that, I glanced over to the porch and noticed now it was all screened in and painted white. It used to be green.

"Wow, I see you enclosed the porch. Looks great," I offered.

"Yeah, I'm actually flipping the house in the next month or two. I bought it about a year ago and completely renovated it– gonna see if I can double my money. Wanna come in and have a quick look?" he offered.

I stood there for a second thinking about this. Did I want to?

"Sure, if you don't mind. I'll have a quick look around," The words spilled out of my mouth before I'd really made my decision.

"I'm Chris, by the way. Sorry, I should have said that already," he said as he held out his hand.

"No problem, Chris. I'm Gary," I shook his hand.

He took me inside, and as soon as I entered, I almost regretted it.

GONE was the pantry in the kitchen. Instead, he had put up a door and turned it into a wash room. No more up and down the cellar stairs with laundry.

The kitchen itself was completely new. There were beautiful countertops, a deep trough, porcelain farmer's sink, and cherry wood cabinets.

GONE were the cabinets that Ma had layered so much paint on over the years that they ended up being a few inches thicker than the originals.

Next was the T.V. room. Ma and Dad had knocked a wall down to make one big room. Now, the wall was back up. Chris said they needed it for an extra bedroom. I found out why later.

Next, we walked into the front, "good" room. The room we'd only spend holidays in or would only get to go in there when we had company. It looked the same except for a new coat of paint. He had put a fresh coat of shellack on the hardwood floor.

I walked over to the corner and smiled.

"Still couldn't get rid of the water and rust stain from the Christmas Tree stand, huh?" I said with a smile on my face. Finally, I thought, something familiar.

He walked over, looked at it and said with a laugh, "that son of a bitching thing—I tried like hell and it wouldn't budge."

Then, we went upstairs. Ma and Dad's bedroom was cleaned up with a fresh coat of paint and the floor was shiny, too. I remembered camping out there on hot summer nights.

The room next to it used to be the room I shared with my brothers. I saw when we walked over to it why Chris had made the extra room downstairs. He had turned this room into a walk-in closet.

It had shelves lining the walls for shoes and for hanging clothes and things. You'd never know this was once a bedroom for three boys. I could still envision the bunk beds just like it was yesterday.

I walked over to the closet, opened it and started to laugh. The new carpeting that had been installed ran all the way into the closet. "Did you do the carpeting yourself?" I asked.

"No, I had it done the minute I signed on the house before I moved in," Chris said, while I continued laughing.

"What's funny?" he asked.

"I'll bet you twenty bucks if you pull up the carpeting in there and lift up the third plank from the left, you will find our collection of *Playboys* we all stole from Mr. Gibson's trash can one summer. We have every month in there for the year of '75, except for April. Mr. Gibson must have liked April."

Chris started to laugh, and we made our way downstairs.

One last spot to see.

He took me down to the cellar. We had so many Haunted Houses down here. So many stolen kisses with girls from the neighborhood.

The cellar was still creepy and musty, but it seemed smaller.

GONE was the huge oil drum our cat once slept on.

GONE was the furnace I used to chase my brothers around to scare them. In its place was a new, modern, streamlined version.

As we walked further into the cellar, I wondered if our secret hiding place down there still had our stuff.

I walked over to the wall, saw the loose rock, and pulled it out. A big grin on my face.

Tucked in the crevice was a Ted Williams baseball card, two marbles, and a cut out pair of boobs from the dirty book page I kept when we had stolen the books from the corner store and blind Pastor James caught us.

Chris laughed and said, "geez, you and your brothers were really something."

I thought about this a minute, and then I said, "yeah, I guess we were."

Finally, we made our way back upstairs and into the kitchen. Just as we were getting ready to leave, out of the corner of my eye, I caught a glimpse of blue.

I walked over to the bathroom door and opened it all the way.

Nothing about this room was different. Not a thing. The blue tiles Dad put in for Ma were still there along with the lopsided floor and the blue tub. It was all the same. It was the bathroom of my childhood.

Over my shoulder Chris said, "yeah, I never got around to fixing that. It's a little lopsided but actually it has pretty good bones. I may leave it alone."

I hoped that he would.

We walked out the back door and I said, "well, Chris, it was nice to meet you. I appreciate you showing me around. I better head home. I'm sure the wife and boys are already wondering where I am with their pizza." I offered my hand; he shook it and we said goodbye.

As I turned the corner at the end of the street, I hit track three on my car cd player and "Ramblin Man" came on. I rolled down the window and stuck my arm out making it into an airplane against the wind. Just like I'd done so many times driving through the back roads of Dracut with Dad after church on Sundays.

I took a long—deep—breath in.

It filled up my lungs. I'm reminded of the smell of stinkweed filling up my nose on those hot summer nights so many years ago.

And it hits me.

Walking through that house, I only saw the new for a moment until the old memories would overtake it. And that is what I'll always remember.

Through old, through new, through good, through bad.

This neighborhood is in my blood.

This house and the memories of the people in it are forever in my soul.

I will never get over this place. *Never.*

As I wipe the tears off my face with the back of my hand, I say out loud—as if someone can hear— "and I thank you, God, for that."

ACKNOWLEDGEMENTS

I have to give a shout out to a few people.

To my husband: I love you and thank you for always supporting my inner thirteen-year-old boy and all of my new re-inventions. Also, thank you for listening to me read every single chapter to you without a single yawn.

To all of my kids (birthed, borrowed, related, and grand): You are all my everything.

To Martha: Thank you for being my constant reader of this book, my defender in life, and the best sister ever.

To my brothers, Danny, David and Darren: Thank you for always being your ridiculous, authentic, honorable and creative selves. To me, you are Men Among Men

To all of my in-laws: Thank you for putting up with "Just the Five of Us." You all know, it really is, the ten of us. We are blessed to have you all in our lives.

To Ma and Dad, so glad we are yours. We love you!

To Liz, Z, and Em: Thanks for the editing and modeling!

And finally, to all of my forever homies: I love and appreciate you all.

ABOUT THE AUTHOR

A.G. Reidy currently lives in New Hampshire with her family, but a piece of her heart will always be in Lowell, Massachusetts.

She continues to re-invent herself, find new projects, and looks forward to planning her next Halloween party with the committee.

She cherishes her time with family and friends. And tries to live in gratitude and live by her mantra: "It's real easy to forget what's important in life...So, don't!"

She thanks you for sharing in this fun adventure with her!

Be kind to each other! dinkweeds forever!

Made in the USA
Las Vegas, NV
22 November 2021

35044580R00102